HOLLYWOOD AND VAIN

Persons this *Mystery* is about—

ALEXANDER "BUSTER" BLADE,

former Hollywood child star of the silent screen known as the Wonder Boy of the Westerns, returns home from the War. He's rented an office suite on the edge of San Francisco's Chinatown as the headquarters for his new private detective agency — Confidential Investigations.

PALOMA LIU TSONG,

Blade's savvy, curvy, part-time secretary and Chinatown exotic dancer believes the emerging medium of television spells the end of pulp fiction magazines and radio shows.

LIEUTENANT LEROY ST. JAMES,

San Francisco PD's star homicide detective is a stylish, narcissistic, Beethoven-loving cop. He used to work with Blade at the SFPD before the War. But now that Blade is a private dick, he won't give him the time of day.

IRIS ASQUITH,

the persnickety frail with a missing husband and plenty of cash to find him, is Blade's new client, whether he likes it or not.

THORNER VON EINSBURG

Monarch Studio's stressed out director of Saturday matinee one-reelers, learned the hard way that working with child actors can lead to a long stay in a padded room.

STAN RAYCRAFT

knows he's the *Call-Bulletin's* best investigative reporter, though his editor disagrees. But Stan elbows in on Blade's case to win back his crime beat at the newspaper.

MR. I. CHING,

Buster Blade's enigmatic Chinese shrink, knows more about Charlie Chan pictures than he knows psychiatry. That doesn't bother Blade, just everyone else.

BOOKS BY RICHARD TORONTO

War Over Lemuria (2013)
Shaverology – A Shaver Mystery Home Companion (2013)
Shavertron – The Mimeograph Years (2013)
Shavertron – The MacPlus Years (2014)
Shavertron – The Lettershop Years (2014)
Shavertron – The Mimeograph Years (2014)
Rokfogo – The Mysterious Pre-Deluge Art of
Richard S. Shaver, vols. 1 & 2 (2014)
Half Past Satan – (2025) (published in 2022 as
The Mind Fuhrer under pseudonym Mace Palmer)
Nudist Camp Confidential (2025)

Hollywood and Vain – A Frisco Detective Mystery (2025)
(published in 2020 as Cold War Hot Lead under pseudonym
Mace Palmer)

Illustrations created with Dalle-3

Design and layout by Lora Santiago

Hollywood and VAIN

RICHARD TORONTO

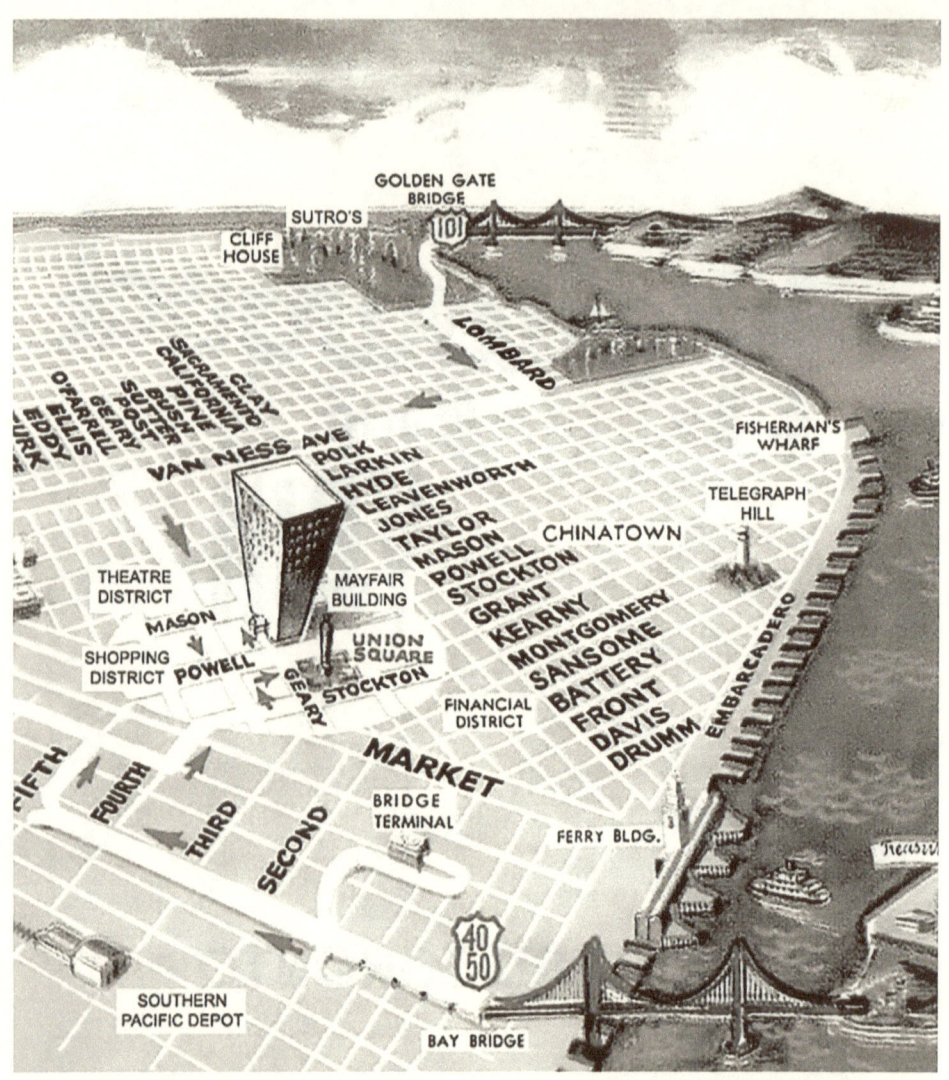

Alexander Blade's San Francisco in 1947

1
The Client

Maybe it was the sea air, or maybe I was just hungry, but that bacon, lettuce, and tomato sandwich made it real hard to concentrate on the new client. I hadn't eaten one of these porcine delights since before the war.

Don't get me wrong. I plowed a few wrinkles across my noggin to let her know I was listening. And whenever she stopped yakking long enough to take a breath, I gave her a sympathetic look that would make any undertaker proud. After taking the last bite of my BLT, I leaned back in my chair, lit up a Chesterfield, and took a good, long look at my new customer.

She was well-preserved and petite, pushing sixty hard enough to raise blisters. Maybe the shapeless black satin dress she wore was the rage in 1929, but she should have ditched it back in 1940. A balding mink stole hugged the old damsel's neck like dead game strapped to the hood of a Kentucky fur trapper's Desoto, but her service stockings hugged a pair of gams that still held their curves. Every movement she made looked like it had been rehearsed in advance, and was quite graceful. I watched her gloved right hand slip into her beaded purse to pull out a pack of Old Golds.

"Not a cough in a carload!" she chirped, parroting the radio jingle.

Call me cockeyed, but it was kind of cute. She could have been a dancer, even an actress on the silent screen in her heyday. She sat straight as a post on the flimsy cafeteria chair while her hand dove back into the purse. This time she produced a cigarette holder, two pieces held together with a rubber band. She assembled it as I watched. It was long enough to poke out my eye when she finished. Removing an Old Gold from the pack, she stuck it into the flared tip of her holder, then clamped her pearly whites down on the business end.

"Got a light?" she said between clenched teeth. It was an odd affectation for an otherwise strait-laced slice of aging femininity. I dug into my coat pocket for a match and obliged her.

She had called my assistant to arrange this chin fest. She wanted to meet me, she said. She might want to hire me, she said. Normally, I meet potential clients at the office, but this one, Iris Asquith by name, preferred Sutro's Automateria. That's where we sat sizing each other up from across our tiny cafeteria table. But beggars can't be choosers. An honest to goodness paying client hadn't darkened my door for a month.

Sutro's was one of those San Francisco landmarks where locals go for a day of cheap entertainment. It's a few doors up from the Cliff House, which, in my opinion had a better, but pricier menu. Just guessing, I'd say the old gal chose Sutro's out of nostalgia. Then again, it may have been for secrecy. The crowds that flock to Sutro's wouldn't think twice about two people flapping their gums in the cafeteria.

Iris Asquith exhaled a plume of Old Gold from the left side of her mouth and continued her monologue.

"You're much too young to remember, Mr. Blade, just how wonderful, how simply *wonderful* Sutro's was before the war. The first war, I mean. Some of the finest vaudeville acts in California performed here. This is where San Francisco's social class came to play in those days. Oh my yes, it was a wonderful place for upper crust San Franciscans to while away the day and be seen."

I replied, "And then the city extended the trolley line and even guys like me came here to play."

My comment dropped a dark cloud over her giddy pan. Her voice faded, like a worn record played too many times with a dull needle.

"Yes, I suppose that is true," she opined.

Like little blue birds, her eyes fluttered from table to table, hoping to land on a familiar face. None were there. A scent of violets, the kind that comes out of little blue bottles from cut-rate drugstores, filled the space around her.

I elbowed into her idle chatter to get the show on the road.

"I was too young to remember the First World War, Miss Asquith."

She jolted, as if she'd sat on a tack.

"*Mrs.* Asquith," she hissed. "Mrs. *Onslow* Asquith."

I nodded. "I beg your pardon, *Mrs.* Asquith. In any case, I spent a big part of my youth here at Sutro's. Saturday mornings my Uncle Jesse would give me two bits to spend as I saw fit. That kept me entertained for an entire day at Sutro's. It cost a dime to get in, five cents to swim in the saltwater pools, and five cents to rent a swimsuit. I bought lunch with the other nickel."

I kept talking to keep her from walking so far down memory lane she'd forget why she was here.

"My Uncle Jesse was captain of the Chinatown Squad. He taught me everything I know about law enforcement. I joined the San Francisco Police Department in 1936, but when the Japs bombed Pearl Harbor, I quit the force and joined the Marines. They shipped me to the South Pacific straight out of camp.

"As you can see, I came home in one piece, more or less. By that time, Uncle Jesse had passed away. So, instead of returning to the force I opened my own detective agency. And here we are."

After such a fine rendering of my autobiography, I rewarded myself with a slug of java so the old gal could ask a few questions. Instead, she sat there in dreamland, puffing on her wheezer like she hadn't heard a word I'd said. She was listening to the sound of organ music and skaters on the ice rink below.

Her Seal Rock Special — tuna salad garnished with tomato, lettuce, and a slice of sourdough, sat there untouched. I watched her poke at it now and then, but she never took a bite. She was adrift on a Sargasso Sea of memories that were ancient history in our new, post-war world of V-2s, A-bombs, and penicillin. Iris Asquith was a female Rip van Winkle who had suddenly woke up in the future of 1947.

2
The Husband

Asquith had been waiting for me at Sutro's Balboa Street entrance. After our salutations, I purchased two tickets and took her arm. Together we descended the steep staircase into Sutro's maze of promenades, ice skating rinks, and sideshow flim flam. The building's mammoth steel and glass structure, a marvel in its day, spanned the entire length of a natural sea cove at Land's End.

The more I thought about it, Asquith and Sutro's were alike, and both were relics of the Victorian Age, and both seemed out of place in the modern world. As we descended into the belly of the vast amusement center, Asquith became my tour guide, like a high school history teacher taking me on a day's outing. Suddenly, she squeezed my arm, mesmerized by a tiny horse carriage. I muttered something about a kids' toy.

"Oh no, Mr. Blade! This was not built for a child," she said, her voice edging up a notch. "This was Colonel Tom Thumb's wedding carriage. Tom Thumb was P. T. Barnum's world-famous circus midget."

"How interesting," I said, as I tried to move her along.

We passed the "Birds of America" display, with stuffed birds chirping in dead silence on bits of twig. Finally, we came to one of my favorite exhibits — the Egyptian mummies. Whenever I came here as a kid I would stand here gawking at the mummies.

Sitting upright in a glass case was the decapitated head of a mummified ancient Egyptian. Next to the head was its, or someone's, desiccated right hand. And they were exactly where I'd seen them 20 years ago. Through the rotting bandages I made out the head's withered eyes and mouth. Its dry, ashen tongue stuck out between its yellow, 2,000 year-old teeth.

I used to make up stories about this head. I called it Ardeth Bey, after Boris Karloff in *The Mummy*. I imagined a time thousands of years ago, when Ardeth Bey rode a camel to see his fortuneteller, an old gypsy woman.

Staring into her crystal ball, the gypsy said, "Ardeth Bey, two thousand years hence, people will pay a dime to gawk at your dried head in a California roadside attraction."

At which, Ardeth Bey replied, "You're nuts! There's no such thing as California."

I'd finished my third cup of Automateria coffee and still had no idea why Iris Asquith wanted to see me. Thanks to copious amounts of caffeine, I began to get testy.

"Okay, Mrs. Asquith, it's been fun hearing your stories, but you're beating around the bush. Let's have it. Why do you need a private investigator?"

From out of nowhere a hanky fluttered in her right hand. It flew up to her mouth to stifle a tiny sob.

"It's my husband," she sniveled.

I interrupted her lament.

"Sorry Mrs. Asquith, I don't take divorce cases."

Her eyelids flapped open like runaway window shades.

"Divorce? Don't be ridiculous! What ever gave you that idea?"

I said: "Nine times out of ten when a wife wants to hire a private detective and 'husband' is the first word out of her mouth, there's another woman waiting in the wings."

"Contrary to your wild assumption, there is no other woman, Mr. Blade. The reason I'm here is because Onslow, my husband, hasn't returned from his annual booksellers' convention in Sacramento. It's been five days now, and I haven't heard from him."

"Five days!" I yelped. "Haven't you filed a missing person report? Have the Sacramento police been notified?"

"Heavens no! Onslow would never forgive me if I involved the police."

"Listen, Mrs. Asquith, I'm not sure where you're from, but here in California most people call the cops when a loved one goes missing for five days."

The pink rouge on her pasty cheeks deepened to red.

"Sometimes Onslow likes to dally after the convention, you know, to follow up on leads to rare book collections," she said. "But he's been gone far too long for that. I suppose I should tell you about Onslow and the police."

"Maybe you should, but is it a long story? I'd like some dessert."

"Don't be so impatient; stay right where you are," she scolded. "You see, Onslow and I were living in Detroit during the Depression years. It was a difficult and dangerous time for assembly line workers in the auto industry, and for reasons too numerous to mention, they began to go on strike. In 1932, Onslow joined the strike at the Ford Motor Company plant in Dearborn. That's near Detroit."

"Should I write this down?"

"Rude remarks do not become you, Mr. Blade."

"Sorry. It's something I picked up during the war," I said. "Would you excuse me a moment?"

I sprinted to the wall of automat doors and thumbed a buffalo nickel into the slot next to a piece of cherry pie. I opened the glass door and retrieved the pie. It looked like it had come straight from the cherry pie slaughterhouse, dripping in red goo.

Mrs. Asquith was puffing her Old Gold when I got back to my chair, pie in hand.

"Excuse the interruption," I said as I cut off the tip of the pie with my fork. "Dearborn is near Detroit?"

"Yes, but that's hardly the point, is it? Where was I? Oh yes, I remember. During the strike, Henry Ford's private police force — goons, we called them — shot and killed several striking workers. After that, Onslow felt so strongly about workers' rights that he joined the Young Communist League. Mind you, it wasn't because he loved Stalin or anything like that. He believed capitalism had become, as Jack London used to say, the iron heel on the neck of the workingman.

"Onslow attended Party meetings every month, hoping to uplift the downtrodden factory worker. He believed he was doing good. You do understand, don't you?"

"Okay, he was a Bolshevik. A lot of working stiffs were in those days," I said. "What's all this got to do with keeping the cops out of a missing person case?"

"I'm coming to that!" she snapped. "Our lives changed forever when Onslow was arrested at a party rally 15 years ago. The League had rented a Detroit ice skating rink for the rally, and it drew thousands of people. But when the police showed up, the crowd got angry. It ended in a terrible row. Three people died, and all YCL party members there were arrested.

"When the police found out Onslow was one of the rally organizers, they gave him the second degree for 12 hours."

"I think you mean the third degree," I said.

"Well, whatever degree it was, they beat him with a rubber hose. They burned his arms and hands with cheap cigars. They told him they didn't like Commies, and he should go back to Russia where he belonged. The judge sentenced him to six months for inciting a riot. That put Onslow on a list of Communist sympathizers, so whenever the police decided to round up 'the usual suspects' they came looking for poor Onslow.

"It was unbearable, Mr. Blade. We moved to California to put the shame behind us, but not before Onslow resigned from the Party. With today's anti-Communist fever, if it's ever found out you were a member of the Communist Party, you're in for a public shaming at the very least. It can ruin your life. I hope now you understand why he avoids contact with police."

"I see. What was your husband doing at this book sellers' convention?"

"Good heavens! You're a detective, Mr. Blade, isn't it obvious? Onslow sells books. He owns the Metaphysical Bookstore on Polk Street."

She reached into her purse for an envelope. Ever so gently she laid the envelope on the table and began pushing it in my direction.

"There is $500 in this envelope," she said. "I hope it will suffice as a retainer."

The envelope looked nice and fat, like it had just swallowed a trout. I peeked inside. It wasn't Confederate money. It looked real.

"That should suffice," I croaked. "Tell me, how did you choose my agency? I don't have a flashy ad in the Yellow Pages or ads running on the radio."

"To be honest, I know nothing about detectives, Mr. Blade, but I like to think I know you quite well," she replied somewhat mysteriously.

"Have we met before?"

"Why, yes, in a way. I expect everyone knows Buster Blade, Wonder Boy of the Westerns," she beamed. "I've seen every one of your pictures, except *Two Guns for Baby Peggy*. You're someone who can get the job done."

3
The Movies

So that was it. Iris Asquith was a fan of my movies, which is something I try to keep on the QT. I prefer a low profile, the reason being that when people recognize me, they either want to ask for an autograph or pick a fight. I prefer to use Alexander instead of "Buster," the name the Hollywood moguls gave me. But Asquith didn't stop there.

"Do you still carry the engraved six shooters William S. Hart gave you in *Tombstone Trailblazers*?"

"Only when I have to shoot a bad guy in a black hat," I mumbled.

She prattled on. "Was Biscuits Brown as funny in real life as he was on the screen? My favorite Biscuits movie is '*Mush Baby Gone.*' That's the one where he and his baby sister Amnesia run away from home to become lion tamers in the circus."

She was like most fans. Over time, movies become as real as the memories of their own lives. But Asquith's walk down memory lane was getting us nowhere fast.

"Let's go back to your missing husband, Mrs. Asquith. Did he give you any indication he might not be coming home? Did he seem depressed or nervous?"

"Not at all. I called the Hotel Ebner; that's where he stays when he's in Sacramento. The manager said he'd seen Onslow on the final day of the convention, but he didn't check out or return his room key. His suitcase is still in his room. The manager said he's holding it for me. It's not like Onslow to leave his things unattended. I've received no calls from him or the authorities, for that matter. He could be wandering the streets in a daze for all I know. You *will* find him, won't you, Mr. Blade?"

"It's against my better judgment to keep the police out of a case like this, but you say there's been no report of your husband's demise, and you haven't received any ransom notes, correct?"

"No, I have not."

"I'll see what I can do. Have you got a recent photo of your husband?"

Iris Asquith was nothing if not prepared. Again, she reached into her beaded purse, this time for a snapshot of Onslow Asquith. She gazed at the photo as she held it in her gloved hand.

"Onslow didn't have a beard when we first met," she explained. "He grew it after we moved to California. He said he didn't want to look like the old Onslow anymore."

She gave me the photo. The man had a beard all right. He had the look of a Bohemian North Beach poet, which seemed to jibe with his pinko past. He looked to be in his mid-60s, wearing Raybans with heavy black frames. He wore a light-colored newsboy cap and shorts. A pullover sweater revealed a bookworm's paunch. Directly behind him I recognized one of the two windmills in Golden Gate Park, facing Ocean Beach. He held a picnic basket in one hand, a beach umbrella in the other.

"We'd been to Ocean Beach that day," the gray quail explained. "Onslow loves windmills, so he asked me to take that picture."

"That explains the windmill," I said, "but to be honest, Mrs. Asquith, the photo isn't much help. With the beard, hat, and sunglasses, he could be any one of hundreds of bearded Caucasian males in San Francisco."

"Yes, I'm sorry. Onslow wasn't too keen on having his picture taken," she apologized. "That's because of what happened in Dearborn. If it weren't for the windmill, he wouldn't have allowed me to take this one."

"Has your husband received threats of any kind recently?"

"No, and before you ask, he didn't gamble, owe any money to loan sharks, or have any horrid habits like alcohol."

"What I'm looking for is something to hang my hat on, Mrs. Asquith. The more information I have, the better my chances of finding your husband. Did he do or say anything out of the ordinary when he left for Sacramento?"

Her forehead cross-stitched a few rows while her eyes rolled from one side to the other. She seemed to lose her train of thought, then got back on track.

"He told me he had an errand to run before he caught the train to Oakland. The bank, I think he said. That was all."

Do you manage your husband's bookstore when he's away?"

"No, that's Berkeley Livingstone. He's Onslow's assistant."

"I'll want to talk to him."

The plump white envelope on the table was making my palms itch. I picked it up and slid it into my inside coat pocket.

"What's Livingstone's address? I'll pay him a visit after he gets off work."

"Well, please don't disturb his mother," she warned. "She's not well."

I wrote down a description of her husband's clothing in my note pad, the name of his bank, Livingstone's address, and the address of the Hotel Ebner. Our meeting over, she got up from the table with her Seal Rock Special uneaten.

Being the gentleman I am, I held her arm as we climbed the staircase to street level, parting ways under Sutro's neo-Spanish twin towers. I lingered as I watched her hobble off, steadying herself on the seawall at Ocean Beach, and disappearing into the amusement park along the Great Highway.

I walked back to my Terraplane 71 Deluxe business coupe parked in front of the Cliff Café and unlocked the door. It was only two o'clock. I had plenty of time before the bookshop closed at five, and the old doll's retainer was burning a hole in my coat pocket. I thumbed the starter button on the dashboard and brought six cylinders to life. The engine roared like a feral cat, just like it did before I put it into storage on December 8, 1941. I drove to Red's Place, where a barstool beckoned.

4
Red's Place

Red's Place was a Chinatown booze oasis at the corner of Jackson St. and Beckett Alley, a half block down from Grant. It was a small bar with a jukebox. Most bars in Chinatown don't have jukeboxes. I stashed my coupe in the alley next to a storefront Buddhist temple and strolled into Red's to celebrate the good fortune nestled in my coat pocket.

Red's wasn't just a bar; it was a hotbed of intrigue, where Chinese locals pass information to undercover agents of the Chinatown Squad. Uniformed cops were never allowed in Red's Place. Chinese citizens were skittish when it came to uniformed cops. They reminded them of the bad old days back in China, when they lived under the iron fist of the Manchu.

Thanks to Red's "no uniforms" rule, it opened up a crack in Chinatown's Wall of Silence. Red's is where plainclothes cops were tipped off to Chinatown crime. The system was simple.

Say a Chinese businessman hears of an impending tong rumble. He doesn't want to be seen at the police station, so he goes to Red's Place for a beer instead. If no cops happen to be there, an anonymous note slipped to the bartender will find its way to a squad member for follow up. No questions asked. It's old school, but it works.

I parked my heft on a barstool and glanced at some plainclothes squad boys soaking up suds at a corner table. Like a pack of spiders, they waited patiently for some disgruntled shop owner to buzz in and finger a *boo how doy* highbinder. One of them must have fed some nickels into the jukebox. It was playing the Mills Brothers.

I ordered a beer to kill time before returning to the office. That's when an unpleasant voice crawled out of my past.

"Well, I'll be damned. It's Buster Blade, has-been of the kiddy Westerns," the voice said.

Magid Batch of the Chinatown Squad perched himself on the barstool next to mine. He was not one of my favorite characters when I worked on the SFPD, and I had doubts he improved with age. Batch joined the Squad in 1934, and knew every gambling den and brothel in Chinatown. The grapevine had him "on the sack," taking protection money from local gambling houses. His round, greasy head sat on a fat helping of jowls, and his food-stained double-breasted suit had never seen the counter of a dry cleaner's shop.

"How long has it been, Buster? Five, six years?"

"It seems like only yesterday," I said between clenched teeth.

The bartender came over to us and Batch ordered a beer. He kept talking.

"I hear you're playing private dick over at the Mayfair building. St. James claims you tarnished your uncle's memory when you turned private peeper."

"That's St. James for you," I said. "He's always got an opinion about something that's none of his business."

Batch took a long pull on his beer. The jukebox swapped records and began to play *Hey! Ba-Ba-Re-Bop*. Still, Batch wouldn't shut up.

"What's it like having a ching-ching China girl as an office assistant," he smirked.

My hands turned to fists and dug fingernails into my palms.

"Better watch your mouth, Magid. It says real stupid things when you're not paying attention."

"Hey, I got no beef, if it rings your bells. Just so she stays on the Chinese side of Stockton Street. Hey, is it true a Chink girl's cootch goes sideways instead of up and down? Or have you got that far with her yet?"

Even the warm glow of 500 clams in my pocket wasn't enough to give Batch a free pass on that one. I glanced over his shoulder at the front door. The jukebox had swapped Lionel Hampton for Frankie Laine.

I acted surprised. "Say, is that St. James?"

Batch spun around on his bar stool to take a look. I stood up.

"I don't see…"

As he turned back to face me, I clocked him. He and the bar stool hit the floor so hard the floorboards bent. He thrashed around like a scoop of mashed potatoes trying to grow legs.

"You fucking bastard! That's assault on a police officer!"

I grinned as he struggled to his feet. That's when I saw his hand go for the revolver under his left armpit. My fist was faster than his. I plowed my knuckles into his flabby gut and he folded in half like a rag doll. I launched an uppercut to his jowls that split his upper lip and put a few stars into orbit around his thick skull.

To his credit, Batch bounced back for Round Two. A rush of adrenalin catapulted him off the floor. With a rebel yell, he lunged forward. I should have pummeled him with all the pent-up rage I brought home from the war. Instead, I moved to the left and watched him ricochet off the bar like a pinball off a cushion. He was back on the floor.

That was when his fellow Squad members came to his rescue. I had worked with them when I was SFPD, and they were okay. They'd been watching in mild amusement as Batch took his licks.

"Now, now boys," one of them soothed as he stepped between us, "cease and desist this cop-on-cop violence. It's bad for the department's image when two white cops carry on like a couple of tong boys. Magid, you were begging for what Blade dished out."

They hoisted Batch off the floor and began to tidy him up. He picked up his hat and slammed it onto his greasy conk.

"You sucker punched me, Blade! These guys just saved your ass, but next time you won't be so lucky. Got that?"

I gave him a toothy grin. "I'll have my Chinese secretary write that down so I won't forget. Have a nice day."

With his pals on either side to steady him, Magid Batch shuffled out the door. A guy can't even order a beer these days without some jerk spoiling it.

5
575 Fell Street

The hands on my tank watch closed in on half past five when I lamped Berkeley Livingstone's wikiup in a row of Victorian cottages, all identical, shoulder-to-shoulder on the 500 block of Fell Street. Apparently, home maintenance was at the bottom of his landlord's To Do list. Its lead paint blistered and flaked off the redwood siding, and its window shades hung in shreds.

I found an empty curb space to stash my heap and walked up to the Livingstone abode. A dime store replica of the Eye of Horus, an ancient Egyptian amulet, caught the bay breeze and spun lazily at the top of the stairs.

Any fortuneteller worth her salt could have told Livingstone that within 15 years this entire block would be razed to make way for a freeway on-ramp. But for now, 575 Fell Street lived on; shedding paint and brooding over better days.

The door had an antique turnkey doorbell engraved with art nouveau flourishes. I turned the key full circle, and to my surprise, it rang. I waited.

A faded lace curtain in the bay window yanked aside as a pale, white face appeared within its dusty halo. The curtain settled back down and footsteps followed. They were not the sound of steady footsteps, more like a step and drag, step and drag, like Lon Chaney's mummy leaving its tomb. The face from the bay window reappeared inside a peephole in the door.

"Yes?" the face said.

"Mr. Livingstone? My name is Alexander Blade. I'm the private investigator Mrs. Asquith hired to locate her husband. Did she tell you I'd be coming around?"

The face disappeared again. I heard several locks unbolting. The door opened a crack and the face squinted at me from behind the door chain.

The face raised an eyebrow. "Mrs. Asquith?"

I flashed my buzzer.

"That's right," I said. "Mind if I come in so we can talk for a few minutes?"

The face drooped in resignation. "I suppose so."

I'd come to expect this kind of lackluster welcome in my line of work. On a popularity scale, the private dick ranks just below the encyclopedia salesman. On the bright side, we're a step up from vacuum cleaner salesmen. Livingstone closed the door to slip off the chain. He opened the door just wide enough to let me slip inside.

I entered a dark corridor. My reticent host began limping ahead of me, leading to what I assumed would be the parlor. His bum leg made the steady dragging sound I'd heard. To my surprise, we were not going to the parlor. Instead, we entered Bela Lugosi's secret laboratory. Well, it was what I imagined Bela Lugosi's laboratory would look like. Now I understood why Livingstone had his wigwam locked up tighter than Fort Knox.

The room was filled floor to ceiling with electronic gadgets. Electrical cords crisscrossed above my head, plugged into the cast iron light fixture that hung from the ceiling. An Oscilloscope and some ham radio equipment gathered dust on a mission oak table.

A ticker tape machine on a metal stand clicked like grandma's false teeth. It spat out an endless paper tongue that filled a beat-up tin wastebasket. Capacitors, resistors, vacuum tubes, transformers, and other electronic gizmos were stuffed into cardboard boxes under tables. A Tesla coil leaned against a worn leather chair near the bay window.

A woman's frail voice drifted in from another room.

"Who is it, Berkeley?" the voice asked. This must be Mother Livingstone, the one Iris Asquith warned me about.

"It's all right, Mother," Livingstone replied. "It's someone who works for Mrs. Asquith. Go back to sleep."

Berkeley Livingstone resembled his house. Stocky, weathered, disheveled, he looked 50-ish, and would have been clean-shaven three days ago. A pair of red suspenders held up his threadbare gray trousers. Their sagging cuffs were full of dried pinto beans. I didn't ask. On top he wore a coffee-stained light blue pinstriped shirt with no collar.

"Wait here," he said, and limped into the kitchen. He brought out a rickety cane chair and placed it in front of me. I sat down and studied the decor. From the look of this place, he was an inventor, or a serious hobbyist.

I heard what sounded like muffled voices coming from a box about the size of a small table radio. A single vacuum tube mounted on top of its steel chassis glowed dimly. Livingstone saw me staring at it.

"That's a Star Mech," he volunteered. "It picks up transmissions from other planets, but I can tune it to pick up conversations from all over the block, too. I'm working on a model that'll fit into my pocket watch."

I leaned closer and listened.

"It sounds like Orson Welles with a mouthful of marshmallows," I observed.

Livingstone seemed anxious to explain further.

"I've determined that one signal in particular comes from an area one hundred and one miles above Duluth, Minnesota. It's called Atmospherea. If you've ever read the OAHSPE Bible, you'll know what I'm talking about. It's thoroughly explained in OAHSPE."

This was indeed a coincidence. Just the other day, my assistant Paloma Liu Tsong had given me a copy of OAHSPE as a belated Chinese New Year present. She explained that if I read all 876 pages, I'd learn the secrets of the Universe. Paloma was a soft touch for California's metaphysical scene. Being half Chinese, she also believed in the I Ching. Not that I hold any of this against her.

With a deft push from his one good leg, Livingstone hoisted himself onto the stool at his workbench. He leaned his elbows behind him on the bench and studied me with his left eye. The right eye stared off into space.

"I'd like to ask you a few questions about your boss," I began. "Your answers could help determine what happened to him."

"Ask away, but I haven't the slightest idea where he is," he said. He had a slight accent, possibly acquired in Oklahoma.

"Does Mr. Asquith have any enemies that you know of?"

"Not to my knowledge, mister – ah, what did you say your name was?"

"Blade, Alexander Blade."

Livingstone's face went from dolefully gray to deliriously gay in an instant.

"Not *the* Buster Blade, of the Indian Alley Gang? The Wonder Boy of the Westerns?"

"Guilty as charged."

"I can't believe it! What're the odds? By gosh and goodnight! My all-time favorite Indian Alley Gang episode is *Peg Leg Buster*, the one where Biscuits and Sparky tricked you into thinking there was a pirate treasure buried under your parents' kitchen floor. They just don't make 'em like they used to! Boy, howdy!"

"Yes, those were the days when they put arsenic on flypaper," I said. "But getting back to Mr. Asquith..."

"I can't get over it; Buster Blade, here, in *my house*. Oh, *Mother*! You won't believe this!"

My interrogation was going nowhere fast. I had to turn things around.

"Mr. Livingstone…"

"Don't be so formal, Buster. Call me Berk."

"Okay, Berk. Now, I'm not saying Mr. Asquith had the inclination, but I have to ask this for the sake of the investigation, understand? Did he have any female friends after business hours, if you get my drift?"

"Heck no, he did not. Say, would you mind if I wheel Mother in here to meet you? She's a die-hard fan of your films like I am."

"Maybe next time, Berk. Please understand, I need this information. It might help locate Mr. Asquith. I'm sure you can appreciate that."

"Yeah, sure. Keep on goin' then."

"Okay, Berk, this is a tough one; do you have any customers of the red persuasion? Socialists, Communists, nudists, vegetarians, things like that?"

"Buster, we get 'em *all* — swamis, fakirs, channelers, dowsers, Satanists, you name it. It's a metaphysical free for all down there."

"Did Asquith ever talk about his past? I mean, before he bought the bookstore?"

"Oh, sure. He was in show biz like you, but not as famous." He glanced over his shoulder at the bedroom door. The old woman's voice was barely audible, but Livingstone heard it through some sort of empathic telepathy.

"No, Mother, we'll be finished here in a few minutes," he barked.

"What kind of show business was Mr. Asquith involved with, Berk?"

"Vaudeville, a magic act. For the big finale he'd disappear, then reappear someplace far off. At least, that's what he told me. I never saw his act, understand. He'd disappear from the stage, show up in front of the theater and walk back in, that kind of thing. He even said he could be in two places at the same time. It was astral projection, like what the space brothers do. You know, the guys in the flying saucers? They've been in all the papers lately."

"Oh. Yeah, flying saucers. I heard about the pilot who saw a V formation over Mt. Rainier. You believe those stories about the flying discs, Berk?"

"What's not to believe? The space brothers have been observing us since before the war, and boy are they pissed. It all goes back to the A-Bomb. They saw what happened to Nagasaki and Hiroshima. They're afraid we're gonna trigger a chain reaction and blow up the whole shebang, you know, the solar system. That's why they're here, to temper our destructive ways and raise our consciousness."

"More power to them, Berk. Even Billy Sunday couldn't do that. Is there anything else you recall about Asquith's vaudeville career?"

"Well, his wife was his assistant; did she tell you that? She wasn't his wife then. That was 30 years ago, back in the 'teens. They got hitched and moved out here to California. Thought they'd make it big in moving pictures like everybody else. It didn't work out, though. They lived in Tarzana for a while. That's where they fell in with a bunch of channelers and mystics. They used to meet once a month at Edgar Rice Burroughs' house to channel a disembodied spirit named Ashtar."

"You mean, *Tarzan of the Apes*? That Edgar Rice Burroughs? I didn't know he was into that stuff."

"Oh, big time, you bet he was, Buster. Mr. and Mrs. Asquith even joined the Rosicrucians. That's when they moved to Frisco. The Rosicrucians have an Egyptian temple over in San Jose. It's not the real deal of course, it's a scaled down replica of an Egyptian temple. It's really a museum with all sorts of ancient artifacts.

"After Mr. Asquith moved up here he bought the bookstore, and everything worked out pretty good. He's been going to that booksellers' convention in Sacramento for the last ten years. There's never been a problem till now."

"Did Asquith have a stage name?"

"Yeah, it was kind of a funny name. He was Mandark, Supreme Master of Magic."

Livingstone swung his good eye in the direction of the Regulator clock on the wall.

"Jeezuz breezes! It's time for Mother's medicine. I hate to cut our visit short, Buster, but duty calls. It isn't every day Hollywood comes to call."

It had been a long day.

6
The Klansman

I drove back to my Telegraph Hill apartment stash, made a ham and cheese sandwich for dinner and got ready to hit the sack. The new case was shaping up, and the vanishing magician angle made it more interesting. I was no closer to finding him, but Asquith piqued my interest now. I turned out the light and began sawing logs as soon as my head hit the pillow.

I was sleeping the sleep of the dead when The Dream came back. It was a recurring nightmare, really, like a sore tooth that flares up when you least expect it. The Dream takes me back to Pasadena, where I was a little squirt on the cusp of my Hollywood career.

We were living on Ohio Street at the Marengo Gardens Bungalow Court, where our front room window faced a large jacaranda tree. I used to spend my time studying the tree's cobalt blue flowers.

The Dream starts out pleasant enough, but turns dark real fast when I hear footsteps, one after another, the sound of Cat's Paw heels on the hardwood floor. They're coming down the hall toward the room where Mother kept me in my playpen. Dread overcomes my pediatric pan as the footsteps get louder. They're coming for me.

I see pages of a huge calendar peel themselves off and fly away like bats. Imaginary months go by, and I can't take my eyes off that damned arch leading into the hallway. Then, the footsteps stop.

That's when the nightmare gets serious.

A ghostly, glowing head peeks around the corner, its hollow eyes fixed on mine. The spook is white as snow. It makes slippery, rustling sounds, like starched bed sheets. The ghost wears a hood. It has no mouth and no nose, just cold, blue eyes staring at me from two holes cut into the cloth.

The head moves ever so slowly under the arch, and I see a body attached to it. The ghost stands upright, its shoulders draped with a red satin cape trimmed in gold. There's a golden cross within a red circle embroidered on its chest. The ghost floats toward my playpen and looms over me. I'm frozen in fear, and too young to know the ghost is the Orange County Grand Cyclops of the Ku Klux Klan! Finally, the ghostly figure speaks.

"What's the matter, boy? Ain't you never seen a ghost before? Wah, ha ha ha!"

There was something oddly familiar about this ghost. Its breath smelled of old cigars and gin, just like Uncle Carl, Mother's boyfriend. Then the ghost began to sing a song, the same one Uncle Carl used to sing, called *Mystic City*. Because he was drunk, the ghost slurred the lyrics. It went something like,

> "Klansmen, Klansmen, of the Ku Klux Klan/
> Protestant, gentile, native-born man/
> Hooded, knighted, robed and true/
> Royal sons of the Red, White, and Blue/
> Owing no allegiance, we are born free/
> To God and Old Glory, we bend our knee."

In variations of The Dream, the ghost played phonograph records on Mother's Victrola. His favorite was an album by The One Hundred Percent Americans.

I am not kidding when I say that my time spent as a Marine in the Jap's Meat Grinder on Peleliu Island didn't scare me as much as this recurring nightmare. I developed a real phobia over it. Unless it's Halloween, never trust a guy in a white sheet.

The Dream dragged on. The ghost was about to sing *A Cross in the Wildwood* when the phone sprang to life with a shattering clang. I grabbed the receiver and croaked, "Blade talking."

"Alex, it's Paloma." The silken voice of my almond-eyed secretary Paloma Liu Tsong sizzled over the wire. She was distraught.

"Heft your hindquarters over here pronto, PI. There's someone in the waiting room you've gotta see right away."

"Jeezuz. I must've overslept. Can they wait?"

"Oh, he'll wait all right. He's as dead as your movie career."

"Great! I don't suppose he died of natural causes."

"Only if he grew that knife in his chest," Paloma replied. "Alex, I'm really creeped out! Put on your trousers and get over here fast!"

I slammed the receiver into its cradle, threw off the covers, sprinted to the bathroom. I gave my Gillette a quick tour of my facial contours, then donned the outfit I wear for dead clients: a dark, worsted-wool double-breasted suit and a light gray Stetson snap-brim hat. Ten minutes later I dropped anchor in front of the Mayfair Building.

The Mayfair was a six-story pile of bricks built around the time Pershing marched into France, with Beaux Arts styling and carved satyrs, all shaggy-haired and hoofed, cavorting along the top story. You can see them if you stand across the street in Burritt Alley and take the time to look up.

The Mayfair's elevator stopped working shortly after the contractor came down with a 10-year case of San Quentin. During the First War, he'd unpatriotically stolen building materials from the Army Presidio. The manager here steadfastly blamed the Second War for putting off repairs. Elevator parts had been requisitioned by the military, he said. I guess he hasn't got the good news yet. That war's been over for the last 18 months.

I climbed the stairs two at a time to the fourth floor. A trail of blood led me to the last door on the left; my door, "Alexander Blade — Confidential Investigations." I swung open the pebbled glass door and piped Paloma at her desk. She looked scared, but that only made her more alluring.

7
Paloma and the Dead Man

Under the circumstances I should have been gawking at the stiff on the chair, not at Paloma. But her gorgeous eyes are jade green, and she was wearing her form fitting wool sweater that hugged those two heavy handfuls of glorious femininity. Her pleated skirt fell just below her knees, and for good luck she'd cinched a red leather belt around her slim waist, accentuating her well-developed hips. This gave her the ever-so-trendy wasp-waisted look the fashion mavens yammer so much about in the fashion columns.

Confidential Investigations was just a part time gig for Paloma. She and her roommate Betty Yim worked nights as chorines at Andy Wong's Sky Room on Grant Avenue. Their shapely gams appeared with the Wongettes, a dance team in the club's Chinese glamour girl review.

I first met Paloma at the Black Cat, a North Beach coffee house. She said she was looking for a safe place to stash her costumes and props, and I had just opened the agency and needed someone to manage the office. So, we made an arrangement. She got the empty room in my office, and I got a part time assistant. She had her own key, with Fridays and weekends off.

In time, she told me how her family went all the way back to Spanish California, when King Carlos IV of Spain gave her great-great-grandfather a massive land grant in the California colony. That was before the gringos took over. After that, great-great-granddad lost everything and the family scattered up and down the California territory.

Her mother, Esmeralda, was working in a Japanese drugstore on the Sacramento delta when she met Paloma's Chinese father, who owned a pear orchard just outside of Isleton. The blend of East and West endowed Paloma with an impressive topography. She developed hills and dales that riverboat captains from Walnut Grove to Birds Landing yearned to explore. But Paloma had other plans.

She'd heard about the booming Chinatown club scene, and the demand for Chinese performers. The clubs had become a major attraction for the post-war flood of San Francisco tourists. So, Paloma skipped her

high school graduation and boarded a riverboat for Martinez. From there she caught the southbound Daylight to Frisco, where she landed a job as a pony dancer, hoisting her pins and bounced her pretties night after night, cheered on by packed houses.

Paloma pointed to the remains and gulped, "Alex! We're in trouble!"

That snapped me out of my reverie. A man hunched over in one of the three captain's chairs. A wide brim felt hat drooped over his forehead. He wore matching brown tweed coat and trousers, darkly stained in blood. A black pool of the stuff, as thick as strawberry preserves, collected on the floor under his chair. He clutched an envelope on his lap, and on closer inspection, I saw my name on it, written in big capital letters that spelled RETAINER.

Paloma shivered. "H-he was s-sitting there just like that when I g-got in."

I said: "This puts me in a tough spot, Legs. I'll have to call Homicide, and that means Leroy St. James."

A slow recognition crawled out of my memory vault as I studied the corpse.

"Hey, I know this guy! This is Bob MacGyver, the Monarch Studios cameraman. He shot all our Indian Alley Gang one reelers!"

I checked inside his coat and found his wallet. It was MacGyver all right. His California driver's license said he lived at 523-B San Gabriel Court in Sierra Madre. He was 55; single, five-feet-eight-inches tall, brown eyes, gray hair. He wore spectacles now.

I removed the manila envelope from MacGyver's death grip. St. James would never find out; besides, it had my name on it.

I emptied the contents onto Paloma's desk. A bundle of greenbacks held together with a rubber band fell out, along with a news clipping from the *Los Angeles Times*. I counted the dough. It totaled $250. The clipping was a two-column inch obit from three months ago that hinted at the purpose behind MacGyver's visit.

July 24, 1947

Former Child Actor Found Dead
The Indian Alley Gang's favorite fat kid, Lazlo "Tubby" Manheim, died of an apparent heart attack in his North Hollywood home Tuesday. A neighbor became suspicious when Manheim failed to put out his garbage can on collection day. Police found the 32-year-old former child actor at his kitchen table face down in a nine-layer cake — German chocolate, according to police. It was determined that Manheim was about to eat the cake when the heart attack occurred.

So, Tubby finally met his match: a chocolate cake. I'd seen him eat more than that in the studio cafeteria on his lunch break. His insatiable appetite became a running gag in the Indian Alley Gang comedies.

In *Tubby's Nightmare*, he ate three chocolate cakes that Lilly Lockhart, the gang's adopted grandmother, baked for the church social. This segued into Tubby's surreal stomachache sequence. Our director, Thorner von Einsburg, was known for his expressionistic film fantasies in the German tradition.

So, Tubby, stuffed with cake, fell asleep and dreamed he'd died and gone to hell for his misdeed. Demons poked and prodded him with tiny pitchforks. The demons were played by the rest of the Gang. They tied him to a spit and were slow roasting him over an open fire when little Stinky snuck up on him at the kitchen table and smacked him with a baseball bat. That's when Tubby's eyes popped open and, he knew it was just a dream. Essentially, these were juvenile morality plays based on the

Seven Deadly Sins, and it looked like real life Tubby paid the ultimate price for Gluttony.

Other than the irony of this untimely death, why did Bob MacGyver want me to see this? The $250 retainer was real money, and that made him a client. I went from zero to two clients in two days. Sure, one of them was dead, but I'm not picky. I grabbed the phone on Paloma's desk.

"Give me police headquarters!" I yeeped.

When the desk sergeant picked up, I asked for Homicide. A few seconds later, an unmistakable voice grated over the wire. The voice was gruff with a slight lisp.

"Homicide, St. James."

"Alexander Blade talking, lieutenant. I've got a customer for you. He's also my client, and he needs your expert attention."

"I don't want to hear about your clients, Blade," he groused. "Why in H are you bothering me with this?"

"Because he's DOA. He's got a serious case of stiletto in his chest."

"Remind me not to ask next time. I'll be there in half an hour. I'm sure it's too late to tell you, Blade, but don't touch anything!"

"Absolutely not, lieutenant."

8
Leroy St. James

Twenty-nine minutes and fifty-seven seconds later, Leroy St. James burst through the office door like a grizzly bear on goofballs. He wore his signature bowler hat, a brown, woolen overcoat, a red bow tie with gold Masonic symbols, and a vest with a silver watch chain dangling from the pockets. The best bootblacks in San Francisco shined his custom-made Italian shoes.

Two of St. James' finest cuts of beef flanked him on either side; his personal bodyguards. They, too, wore overcoats, but opted for Knox Westlite hats with a bound edge; a solid choice for a ten-dollar hat.

St. James was a human A-bomb in a constant state of fission. He filled a room with dangerous levels of radioactive crime fighter within seconds. God had chosen St. James to catch perps and give them a one-way ticket to the gas house. That's what St. James thought, anyway.

He was heavyset, maybe 245, six feet, with a face of yeasty, white dough. Under that derby hat he was as bald as a baby's elbow and his 50-something countenance was strangely infantile; yet somehow it managed to grow a bristle mustache. He wore round, tortoise shell specs that gave him the look of a Sansome Street accountant.

St. James molded the world to fit his personal point of view. It was his belief that he had been Ludwig van Beethoven in a previous life.

As Beethoven, he put secret messages between the lines of his symphonies so that his 20th Century incarnation would find them. When St. James wasn't sport fishing on the Sacramento River, he was decoding these secret messages, one of which, he believed, was a cure for deafness.

To be fair, this was just the office scuttlebutt, tidbits of gossip making the rounds at the SFPD. But if you worked around St. James long enough, the rumors began to make sense.

St. James barked orders to his blue minions. Seal the office! Comb it for clues! Call the coroner! Get some coffee! MacGyver's hunched remainders seemed of little interest to him, and he went straight to

Paloma's desk. Her abundant charms had no effect on St. James, who got straight to the point.

"Okay China girl, where's Blade? I've got two more stiffs waiting for me, and my stomach feels like an elephant just took a crap in it. It's that damn egg foo young I had for breakfast. Well, what are we waiting for, let's go! Chop chop, ching ching!"

St. James' surly demeanor belonged to the alter ego he invented as chief of the Homicide Squad. He played the part of the infallible lawman, and was pretty good at it. His bull-in-the-China-closet approach to crime made big headlines wherever he went, and he wasn't shy about blowing his own horn.

I got up from my Navy surplus swivel chair, snubbed out my Chesterfield, and brushed the cigarette ashes off my coat sleeve. There was really no need to make a good impression on the lieutenant. We knew each other long before the war. He and Uncle Jesse had been fast friends. On occasion I worked with St. James when I was still on the force, but now, as a private cop, I was invading his turf.

"Never mind me," I said as I ankled into the room. "How's business, lieutenant?"

"Business is fantastic, Blade. And do you know why? Armageddon. The blood-sucking vampires are reproducing like fruit flies. If I don't drive a stake through their shriveled black hearts they just keep multiplying. They're like the damn Commies!

"So this is where it all happens," he said with a sneer. "You call this flop house a detective agency? If your uncle were still here this would break his heart, you know that, don't you? His dying wish was to see you back on the force. But no — you had to be a private snoop. I guess that's all water under the bridge, eh, Buster?"

He reached into his coat pocket for his note pad, then laid the icy copper's swivel on me.

"Okay, give it to me from the top, Philo."

"His name is Bob MacGyver," I droned. "He was a cameraman when I worked at Monarch Studios. He filmed all our one-reelers. Paloma found him just like this when she got to the office at nine o'clock."

"Ah, that's right," St. James continued in a derisive tone. "How could I forget? You were a Hollywood brat! And yet, I don't recall seeing your footprints on a concrete slab at Grauman's Chinese."

"Hey, they'll come begging for them one of these days," I griped. "In any case, MacGyver was going to hire me with this $250 retainer." I passed the manila envelope to St. James.

"You'll note my name written on the envelope. Before he could hand it over, somebody slipped a shiv between his ribs. From the trail of blood in the hallway, I'd say he was lucky to get this far."

"A great place to end up, too" St. James egged. "Why would this guy want to hire you?"

"Maybe I'm good; maybe because he knew me; or maybe because of this newspaper clipping. It was in the envelope along with the lettuce."

"Didn't I hear myself say something to you about not touching anything, or did I just imagine it?"

"The envelope was addressed to me. I opened it. Other than that, he's in as found condition."

St. James took the clipping, scanned it, and remarked, "Okay, an obese, out of work 32 year-old kid actor has a heart attack. What's in this that's got anything to do with your dead client?"

"Dunno. I worked with Tubby when we were kids. Other than that, I can't say. But that $250 retainer makes MacGyver a client, and I intend to find out."

St. James' face opened in a grin that showed the gap between his upper front teeth.

"Bad news, Buster; your windfall just became police evidence. But don't fret, you'll get a receipt; maybe even get it back one day."

The coroner walked in complaining to St. James how he interrupted the best poker hand he'd had in years. Then he began to study MacGyver.

St. James's boys were practically scraping the paint off the walls looking for clues, but found nothing. Meanwhile, a police photographer arrived with his Speed Graphic. He fired off a few flash bulbs that turned the two paint scrapers into sinister shadows on the wall.

Paloma recited the lieutenant her statement, detailing the time she arrived at the office, confirming again that she'd left everything untouched.

"I reckon the time of death to be about five o'clock this morning, lieutenant," the coroner wheezed through the cigarette in his chops. "That means he'd been here four hours before this young lady arrived on the scene."

St. James whispered a few words to the coroner. He was running late and anxious to leave.

He turned to me and asked: "Any ideas about the perp who slipped the shiv into him?"

"Cripes, lieutenant," I yelped. "The last time I saw Bob MacGyver I was seven years old. He never sent me a Christmas card, never called to wish me happy birthday. There was no contact between us until now. Long story short, I haven't got a clue. At least, not yet."

St. James prided himself in solving one hundred percent of the cases that came his way. Like Sherlock Holmes, he was the world's greatest detective. He slipped a cigar out of his coat pocket, bit off the end, spat it on the floor and lit a match to it. He exhaled over the corpse. By now MacGyver was under a blanket, strapped to a gurney. Two orderlies in white coats wheeled him down the hall and all four flights of stairs to the meat wagon double-parked on Bush.

Then St. James began to grumble loud enough for everyone to hear.

"This was supposed to be my day off, dammit! I should be on my boat, fishing for bass on the Sacramento. I haven't even tried out my new pole!"

He turned to me and said, "You'll be around if I need you, right, Philo?"

"You know where to find me, lieutenant. Here's my card."

He held the card up to his face until grooves of disdain spread across his lardy map. He slipped the card into his pocket, along with his detective note pad.

"Okay, let's get the hell out of here," he growled "There's a pawnbroker in the Mission with his head bashed in, and a dame that's been strangled by her wop boyfriend in North Beach. The vampires are working overtime, boys!"

St. James left as abruptly as he'd arrived, and the office was as silent as a tomb.

9
Onslow Asquith

Onslow Asquith kept his money in a bank on the corner of Market and Powell. I had a contact there; a teller I'd dated a few times named Francie Ferris. I was hoping we were still on good terms. She might have some dope on my missing bookworm, or would know someone who did.

At the Embarcadero I boarded a Market Street trolley and that gave me time to think. Onslow Asquith made a living by disappearing. Maybe old habits die hard.

I disembarked at the Powell Street stop. Arranging myself on the bank's granite steps, I waited for the Ferris frail to bolt from the bank. It was noon by my tank watch, and Francie always took her lunch break on the dot. True to form, she rushed out the big bronze doors at 12:02. I flipped my butt to the curb and moved in.

"Hi, sweet stuff. Long time no see."

"Well if it ain't Buster Blade, Wonder Boy of the Westerns and all-around crumb."

She must have taken her tonsils out of the freezer when she said it. I guess I wore out my welcome.

"How long has it been, Alex?"

"According to my eidetic memory, it was Labor Day, 1946, the Year of the Dog. We shared a number seven and a pair of chopsticks at Sam Woo's. How could I forget?"

She parried. "In case you hadn't noticed, Alex, it's 1947, the Year of the Pig. You know what a pig is, don't you, Alex?"

"I prefer Year of the Boar."

"Boar, shmore, it's still a pig. Saaay, wait a minute. Is this just a happy coincidence or is there more to this reunion than meets the eye? Whatever it is, you buy lunch. I don't have much time."

"You know me so well it's scary, Francie."

I put my arm in hers and we crossed the street to the Owl Drugstore, dodging a cable car on the Powell Street turntable. I stuck with mindless chitchat until we reached the lunch counter, where the Market Street lunch crunch was in full swing. We were lucky. Two Macys cashiers finished their lunch and we snagged their seats.

A waitress with more curves than the Pacific Coast highway came over to take our order. She filled her outfit like a puffer fish in a straitjacket. A badge with the name "Bev" floated hypnotically above her billowing breastworks. With the quick and deliberate movements of a seasoned waitress, she slid two glasses of water and two straws in front of us.

"Our special today is Salisbury steak with herbed mashed potatoes, hon." Bev's salutation was an impressive display of efficiency; a greeting and menu item all in one.

Francie put down her menu and said, "I'll have the Monte Christo, heavy on the mayo, side of coleslaw and a Coke, please."

The buxom hash slinger swung her name badge in my direction.

"And what would you like, sir?"

My thoughts wrestled with that outfit of hers. Maybe she put on a few pounds after she bought it. Then again, she could have borrowed a friend's uniform and the friend was a size smaller. Inquiring minds wanted to know.

"Ouch!" Francie's elbow jabbed my side. I realized the winsome waitress craved an answer. I ordered black coffee and a cruller. "Old fashioned, if you have one," I said.

"You got it, hon." Bev spun on her Red Wings and beat it to the kitchen window where she clipped our order on a metal wheel. A cable car bell outside the window brought me back to the point.

"Francie, do you know an Onslow Asquith? He has an account at your bank."

"I see," Francie replied knowingly. "Well, since we're on this swell lunch date and everything, yes, I know Mr. Asquith. He comes to my window every week to make a deposit in his business account. I think he has a crush on me." She winked as her tongue snared the straw in her Coke, pulling it between her fire engine red lips.

I ignored Francie's tongue metaphor and asked her: "Did you see him at the bank last week?"

"As a matter of fact, I did, but not at my window. Mine is number seven. He went to number ten, Margie's window. I was miffed at first, since he's been one of my regulars forever. I thought maybe I'd said something that upset him, but I couldn't imagine what. He didn't even look my way. When he left, I asked Marge what he wanted. She said he withdrew a thousand dollars from savings."

Bev returned with our orders. With pinpoint precision she swirled our plates in front of us. "Monte Christo, heavy on the mayo; coffee and an old fashioned. Enjoy, hon."

I watched Bev haul her hindquarters down the line to refill a bus driver's coffee mug. That's when Francie's last words goosed my gray matter.

"A thousand bucks?" I said, as I dipped my donut in my coffee. "That buys a lot of bookmarks."

Francie was only half listening as she wolfed down her sandwich. I craved to hear more. This time, I added a note of concern.

"His wife said he went to Sacramento several days ago and hasn't been heard from since. She's worried sick."

"And you think something's happened to him," she said, her mouth full of coleslaw.

"His wife does. Do you remember what day of the week you saw him?"

"Oh gosh, I don't know, maybe it was a week and a half ago. He usually comes in on Fridays, so it must have been a Friday. No, come to think of it, it wasn't Friday because I had Friday off that week, so it must have been some other day."

"In other words, you don't remember."

"Sorry, hawkshaw. All I can tell you is he hasn't been back since he withdrew that cash."

She raised her Lady Timex and gave it a glance.

"Cripes, I'm down to the wire, Buster. We gotta go."

I paid the counter cutie, or rather, Iris Asquith paid. I'm sure Iris wouldn't mind if I slipped a love token under my plate for Bev. After returning Francie to the bank with a solemn promise to give her a call, I flagged my Florsheims to California Street and climbed aboard the cable car grinding its way uphill. The car made its usual stop at Grant, where I disembarked in front of St. Mary's Church, in the heart of Chinatown.

I loitered awhile to listen to a Chinese street musician play his fiddle. It sounded like a scalded cat. When my ears began to bleed I dropped a nickel in his fiddle case, leaving him to torment someone else. I hiked another block to Stockton, hung a left, walked under the Stockton Street tunnel and climbed the stairs to Bush. The Mayfair Building was still there, whether I liked it or not.

10
The Hotel Ebner

As I stepped into the office, I found Paloma clipping a pair of black nylons onto her red garter belt. Being in show business, she was no shrinking violet. Nonetheless, I pretended not to look.

As she was smoothing down her skirt I announced: "Just to let you know, Legs, I'm driving to Sacramento today. I want to check out Asquith's last known whereabouts and snag that suitcase he left. I should be back around sundown. The MacGyver case has to go on the back burner while I make some headway on Asquith."

I descended the Mayfair's four flights of stairs to saddle up the Terraplane napping in a parking space a block down Bush Street. Crossing the Bay Bridge, I drove to El Cerrito and pulled into a service station for a fill up. The attendant gave her the works. He topped up the tank with ethyl, cleaned the windshield, checked the dipstick, and checked tire pressure. I was ready to roll.

Highway 40 was my quickest route, but it snaked through every hick town between here and Sacramento. Two hours and four Chesterfields later I was crossing the Sacramento River Bridge. The state capitol building glowed like the white castle in Oz, surrounded by swaying palm trees.

In stark contrast, the Hotel Ebner was in Sacramento's West End, the nice word for skid row. The Gold Rush built the West End in its heyday, but Californians being who they are, they craved something bigger, better, more. They never stay put, and that's what happened to the West End. When the gold mines petered out, the money moved on and the winos moved in.

The West End hit the skids in a big way when the war ended. Steamboats that used to make regular stops here disappeared. Cars were the big thing now, and everybody wanted one. Riverboats were left to rot in the muddy sloughs along the delta. The West End became a shady red light district for hookers, booze, and seedy hotels.

The Ebner was a high-class joint once. Now its wrought iron balconies sagged, and the sign above the door was barely legible. It was a low-end flop, offering cheap rooms for field workers, hopheads, and lost souls circling the drain of despair. The lobby still had its black walnut wainscoting, but it was scarred from years of idle hands with pocketknives. Its once grand staircase led to a second story surrounded by balustrades. Smoke and dust dulled its gold leaf ceilings. The air was thick and fusty.

I found the front desk but no clerk. The pigeonholes behind the counter were jammed with old newspapers, beer cans, and single shoes seeking a mate. A folded cardboard sign on the marble countertop read: "Manager in Room 1. Knock and be patient." The sign was written with a shaky hand, someone with the DTs.

Room 1 had a brass doorknocker in the shape of a miniature gold pan with a pick and shovel. The crisscrossed pick and shovel lifted and struck the pan. I lifted it and knocked three times. No reply. I pounded on the door five more times with a clenched fist.

The door opened just enough to make me feel unwelcome. A short, barrel-chested man wearing a cravat and smoking jacket gave me the stink eye. His skin was pink. His hair was red and thinning. Freckles splattered his face like raindrops. He smelled of overripe fruit.

The pink man hovered nervously in the doorway, like a flamingo guarding its nest. His cautious blue eyes sized me up from under puffy pink lids.

"Yeesss?" he hissed. The word hung in the stale air like a soap bubble. Birds twittered in the room behind him. Finches maybe.

I pulled out my buzzer and leveled it with his pink pan.

"I'm looking for a man who stayed here a couple weeks ago," I began. "His name is Asquith, Onslow Asquith, a bookseller from San Francisco."

Mr. Pink's eyes glazed over as they fixed on my gold badge. He was slow to respond, as if the badge was a magnet, pulling him into a sea of woe and tribulation. I glanced over his shoulder into the room behind him. A longhaired man in his twenties, wearing denims and an unbuttoned white shirt lounged on a Victorian velvet sofa. Reefer smoke hung in the air.

"Wellll," Mr. Pink finally uttered, "Mr. Asquith has lodged with us several times for the booksellers' convention, but I can't tell you much more than that. He left without returning his key. I'd say that was about a week and a half or two weeks ago at most. I've told his wife about the suitcase, since he hasn't been back to pick it up. We can only hold it for 30 days; house rules."

"I understand," I said. "His wife hired me to find out what's happened to him. He hasn't made contact with her since he left this hotel. If his room is still vacant, I'd like to see it if you don't mind."

The manager pulled a handkerchief from his jacket to mop sweat off his brow.

"I really don't know if I..." Before he could say no, I slipped a sawbuck into the pocket where his hanky should have been.

"Well, if you think it might help," the pink man said. "Wait here, please."

He closed the door. I heard muffled voices inside the room. One of them belonged to the young man. He sounded angry. There was an argument, then, all was quiet. Mr. Pink reappeared.

"Follow me, pleeeese."

We climbed the grand staircase to the second floor, up another flight of stairs, then down a hall with barely enough light to see numbers on the doors. Outside, a locomotive sounded its air horns as it crossed the E Street Bridge. I heard a radio down the hall playing *Hey! Ba Ba Re Bop*. Someone in Room 32 snored like a moose with swollen tonsils.

The pink man pulled a key from his smoking jacket, he used it to open the door to Room 33, and we stepped inside.

"We haven't gotten around to cleaning the room yet," Mr. Pink confessed.

"Funny," I said. "The bed doesn't look like it was used."

Mr. Pink was in a hurry and did not reply.

"Be that as it may," he said, "the suitcase is in the closet. Lock the door and return the key when you're finished." He dropped the key into my hand, spun around and dashed off down the hall like the White Rabbit into its rabbit hole.

The window in Room 33 faced Firehouse Alley and the river levee beyond. It would be stifling in here without air conditioning during Sacramento's long hot summers. From the look of his room, Onslow Asquith was a thrifty lodger. With a thousand clams in his wallet, he could have done far better.

The wrinkled floral wallpaper looked as though someone had put it up during a monsoon, and the only amenities were a sink, a nightstand with a radio that accepted dimes, and a table with two pressed-back chairs. The double bed with blue chenille bedspread looked unused.

The suitcase was here, just as the pansy said. It was well-used luggage, with an orange Lucite grip. I pushed the two clasps with my thumbs and popped it open. Other than a few items of clothing, some toiletries, and a ten-day-old copy of the *Sacramento Bee*, there was nothing much to see. I folded the newspaper and slipped it into my coat pocket.

I pulled out the elastic pocket in the lid and found a Southern Pacific train schedule. Sacramento's SP station was less than a mile from here on I Street. With a thick lead pencil, someone had circled a train leaving Sacramento at 7 AM, arriving in Santa Cruz later that day. But why would Asquith leave his suitcase? It was beginning to look like foul play. I closed the luggage, turned off the light, and stepped out into the corridor.

The stairs groaned under the heft of my six foot three, 220-pounds. Standing at the manager's door, the argument I'd heard earlier was building a head of steam. Glass shattered. Birds screeched. Mr. Pink let out a yelp. The door flung open and the longhaired man plowed through in a huff. The pink man groveled pathetically behind him, a pained look on his sweaty mug. Neither of them seemed to notice me.

"Don't go, Lance!" the pink man blubbered. "I'm sorry. Here's the money."

"Shut up," spat long hair. "Buy birdseed with it!"

He stormed through the lobby and out the front door. The pink flamingo fluttered back to his nest for a good cry behind his gold miner's doorknocker. I slipped the key under the door and found my way out.

What a world, what a world.

Out on K Street, the Terraplane snoozed warmly a half block away. I'd already taken off my coat out of respect for the heat. I climbed in and thumbed the starter. The Terraplane's twin carbs sucked in the humid, delta air. I cruised to the end of K Street, turned left on Front, and crossed the River Bridge heading for home.

I lit a gasper and cursed the bookworm for not leaving better clues. On the other hand, Bob MacGyver, my dead client, had given me at least one — Tubby Manheim's obituary and his run-in with the chocolate cake. Maybe St. James was right. I should have stayed with the SFPD.

11
Yarrow Stick Warning

I scanned Onslow Asquith's *Sacramento Bee*, found nothing of interest, and hunkered down behind my war surplus desk to mope. I'd purchased the desk, and the rest of my office furniture, from Smilin' Sam's Army-Navy Surplus in the outer Richmond. The government can't get rid of this stuff fast enough, and sells it for pennies on the dollar. If I had wanted to start my own airline I could have bought a fleet of DC-3s, cheap.

It was Paloma's day off, but she was here anyway, waiting for the local television station to sign on. She was killing time by arranging her Chinese yarrow stalks, a kind of Oriental divination. She called it her hand dance meditation.

I'd watched her do this yarrow stick bit before, but it never made sense to me. I'm an Ouija board man, myself. Tossing Asquith's *Bee* in the wastebasket, I wandered out of my inner sanctum to see what she was up to.

"What's the score, Moon Cakes?"

No response. Paloma was beginning her meditation. She pulled a single stick from the jar of 50 and laid it crossways in front of her.

She looked up at me. "This is the Wu Chi stalk," she said, as if I'd understand. "It stands for the unchanging ground of Being. Got it?"

"Yes," I said, "but there's no guarantee after stick number two."

"Okay, watch closely," she said.

She began to separate the sticks into different piles, counted them three different times, and repeated the ritual at least that many more times.

"You've got that blank look on your face again, Alex," she said as she picked up a small pile of sticks. "Now, I put this bundle of stalks in my right hand and separate them into groups of four, just like I did with the left hand bundle."

I said, "Just ask them where I can find Onslow Asquith. Can you do that for me?"

"The yarrow stalks don't care what you *want*, Alex, they tell you what you need to *know*."

"Don't they have a *Readers Digest* version for clueless Occidental bozos like me?"

I lit a Chesterfield. As Paloma wrapped up the ritual, the sticks formed a hexagram. She looked worried.

"The yarrow stalks say you are in danger," Paloma said in a serious tone. "A ghost from the past is returning to haunt you."

Whether the warning was legit or not, the sticks were right about one thing. My past could haunt a Nob Hill mansion.

12
Hollywood

I'd barely blown out the candles on my third birthday cake when Mother began the weekly ritual that would change my life forever. She would take me on the Red Line streetcar from Pasadena to Hollywood for her vigil at the gates of movie studios along Gower Gulch, where, according to the movie magazines, directors picked actors off the street like flowers from a garden. On Tuesdays we stood in front of Altamount Pictures. Wednesdays you'd find us in front of Monarch Studios, and on Thursdays we would stand patiently in front of Hollywood Classics. These were the "Poverty Row" studios along Gower, just off Sunset Blvd.

Mother spent endless hours perfecting my "look," finally settling on the scruffy, mop top toddler in suspenders, bulky knit sweater, and newsboy cap; the Jackie Coogan image Charlie Chaplin made famous in The Kid.

It was 1919, on one of those glorious, blue-sky days you see pictures of in the California travel brochures. We were standing at the front gate of Monarch Studios, and Mother was holding my tiny mitt so I wouldn't wander off. Like all the other stage moms waiting there that day, Mother hoped I would land a bit part to launch my career on the silver screen.

Mother's persistence paid off when the man who would become my director, Thorner von Einsburg, rode up to Monarch's main gate in his chauffeured Lincoln town car.

As the chauffeur exchanged pleasantries with the security guard, Mother and I watched von Einsburg through the window of his limousine. He was fitting a smoke into his cigarette holder. As he did so his gaze drifted out the car window. He sized up the knot of Hollywood hopefuls until his eyes came to a screeching halt on me. We read his lips as he told his driver: "Let me out!"

The lacquer-haired Latin chauffeur wore highly polished riding boots and a powder blue chauffeur's uniform that was custom cut to his slim waist. He placed a mat under the rear door to protect von Einsburg's hooves on the pavement.

Mother and I were frozen in a kind of trance, mesmerizing on von Einsburg heading our way. It felt as though the earth had stopped turning. Neither of us said a word as the other mothers, with toddlers in tow, rushed von Einsburg to give him a look at their offspring. He ignored them all, and spoke only to Mother, studying me all the while.

"What is the child's name, Madame?" he said, adjusting his monocle.

"Alexander, Mr. von Einsburg. Alexander Blade." Of course Mother knew who he was. She'd seen his picture in the movie magazines. She memorized their pages every month with religious fervor.

Von Einsburg turned to me. He looked like a mountain with epaulets.

"Hello, Alexander," he said with a strange accent. "How are we today?"

"Who wants to know?"

The Kraut cracked a Cheshire cat's grin. Mother, on the other hand, looked distressed.

"I'm sorry, Mr. von Einsburg," Mother apologized. "Alex is just a bit tired from standing here all morning."

"A delightfully precocious young man," he said. "You must be very proud." At that, von Einsburg pulled out his card and began writing on the back with a Japanese enameled fountain pen plucked from his military style jacket.

"Give this to the guard at the front gate at exactly one o'clock today," he said. "He will direct you to my bungalow. Be prompt. *Auf vedersehen*, Madame."

He clicked his heels, Prussian style, and climbed into his big, black Lincoln. It sailed under the Monarch Studios arch, leaving the heady stench of high-octane exhaust in its wake.

Mother was happier than I'd ever seen her. We had three hours to kill before our appointment, so she took me to a nearby Owl drugstore. We sat at the soda fountain, where she ordered two chocolate milk shakes. The soda jerk served them in iced parfait glasses. Whatever was happening, I liked it.

The rest of the story, as they say, is history. We met von Einsburg in his bungalow on the Monarch Studios lot. He offered me a part in his latest one-reeler, *Baby Makes Three*, with Ben Turpin. My part was the cute but devious brat in an oversize diaper. The plot was simple. Turpin's overbearing wife puts him in charge of Baby while she visits her sick sister in Venice.

There were plenty of sight gags, with me setting up Turpin for a fall at every turn. Von Einsburg liked my performance so much he cast me in the sequel, *That's A Lotta Baloney*, again as the annoying rug rat.

Monarch signed me to a five-year contract, and that's when I got my movie moniker, "Buster."

Bud Crossman was president of Monarch Studios in those days. He was so happy with our last two comedies that he offered von Einsburg a new series – The Indian Alley Gang — about a pack of precocious kids from a typical American neighborhood in a typical American town. The plan was to shoot on location on the outskirts of Los Angeles. It was cheaper than building sets on the lot. Uncle Bud, as we kids used to call Crossman, cast me as one of the Gang.

It was a cush job. We got more ice cream than we could eat in our wildest dreams. We never went to school because we had private tutors three days a week. Adoring fans sent us thousands of letters, and studio secretaries sent replies with signed publicity photos. We wore expensive clothes and went to swell Hollywood garden parties with other Hollywood movie kids from other studios.

In Hollywood, there is always a downside. Our parents were deathly afraid to let their little moneymakers mingle with the riff raff. Doing so might mean bad press, or we could break our necks, or — heavens to Murgatroyd — fall victim to kidnappers. We might even figure out there was more to life than acting in the galloping snapshots to support good old mom and dad, who lived the Hollywood highlife and paid for it with our salaries.

13
The Ignominious Death of Brick Bannister

Von Einsburg cranked out enough one-reel comedy shorts to sink a battleship. He did so in record time, too. Poverty Row called these films Five-Day Wonders, but von Einsburg broke that record when he knocked it down to just three days. Our gravy train ran off the rails in 1924, when hypertension got the best of him. Tinsel Town gossip rags covered his nervous breakdown in all its gory details. Anyone who knew von Einsburg could tell you he had been building up to it for months. The final crack in von Einsburg's eggshell came during a scene in the ill-fated epic, *Baby Bwana*.

Monarch Studios kept a small zoo of animals on the back lot. It wasn't much, just a few moth-eaten attractions from a circus that hit the skids. Jungle epics were all the rage in those days, so when Uncle Bud heard a certain circus was on the auction block, he outbid all contenders and got the whole menagerie.

Uncle Bud hired an animal trainer named Joe Martin to care for his zoo. Martin managed a bear, a lion, a tiger, various talking birds, an elephant named Mr. Jumbles, and the star of the show, an over the hill chimpanzee named Brick Bannister, who co-starred in every jungle serial Monarch Studios ever produced. He was featured in a number of Indian Alley Gang shorts, too. His piano key grin was a hit among our juvenile fans.

Meanwhile, Hollywood chipped away at von Einsburg's mental mobility. The studio's grueling, non-stop shooting schedule didn't help. Another problem was von Einsburg's cast of somewhat difficult kid actors. Monarch's PR department began touting *Baby Bwana* as Hollywood's greatest juvenile jungle epic. Von Einsburg was in a pressure cooker, and, as usual, Uncle Bud demanded a quick turnaround.

They cast Biscuits Brown as the wild-eyed chieftain of a jungle village. I was a mini version of Tarzan. Carla Darla played a professor's daughter who survived when their plane crashed in the jungle. She became a white princess, rescued and eventually worshipped by the local tribe. Swifty, Tubby, Stinky, Amnesia, and Sparky played themselves.

Being a jungle epic, *Baby Bwana* needed a supporting cast of jungle animals, which meant von Einsburg had to tap into the studio zoo. He was about to shoot the scene where I would ride Mr. Jumbles into a native village to rescue Carla Darla from a group of evil white men who wanted the oil and mineral rights to her kingdom. They were holding her for ransom, and natives from a rival village were in cahoots with the evil white men.

Brick Bannister may have had a winning smile on screen, but behind the camera he was as mean as a gorilla with a sore tooth. He needed constant pampering from his keeper Joe Martin. On the day of the big scene, Brick must have gotten up on the wrong side of the bed. He was in a mood most foul, thanks to Joe Martin, who had rushed him onto the set before his usual breakfast of plantains and Cracker Jack.

Mr. Jumbles was already on the set. I was waiting in the wings to come running up to Mr. Jumbles, climb onto his back, and forge ahead to save Carla Darla. Brick Bannister wore his signature leopard skin cave man outfit. He was supposed to ride with me on top of Mr. Jumbles. The other kids were in their places and ready to go. Von Einsburg shouted "Speed!" "Camera!" "Action!"

I climbed aboard Mr. Jumbles, but Brick Bannister froze. The goofy gorilla's gray matter went haywire. That's when all hell broke loose.

Brick was standing next to Joe Martin when, in one quick move, the ape grabbed Martin's loaded Smith & Wesson from his holster. Gat in hand, Brick scampered up a light stand where he began blasting lead pills at us. Everyone ducked for cover, but only one shot found its mark.

Mr. Jumbles, who'd been placidly grazing near von Einsburg in the director's chair, reared up as monkey lead pierced his rear flank. Standing on his hind legs, the animal reached an astounding height. I dove for safety, falling through the thatched roof of a native hut. But von Einsburg did not move. He was paralyzed with fright. Mr. Jumbles was just about to turn the director into sauerkraut when Joe Martin raised his long gun and blazed fire at the raging pachyderm. Sadly, Mr. Jumbles dropped dead on the spot. Von Einsburg was saved.

Martin then turned his attention to the devil ape. While everyone was looking at poor Mr. Jumbles, Brick Bannister had climbed a fake palm tree and began pummeling cast and crew with plaster coconuts.

I've heard that if you sit a chimp in front of a typewriter, it will eventually type a real word. The same is true for an ape with a gun. After firing five shots blind, and with one round left in the chamber, the

malevolent monkey took steady aim and blew a hole in his keeper's left shoulder. This enraged Joe Martin.

KA-BOOM! A blast from Martin's long gun blew Brick Bannister out of the palm tree into the window of the Bucket of Blood Saloon on a Western set 50 feet away.

During the melee, von Einsburg suffered a broken arm, but the real damage was inside his head. Brick Bannister had tossed the proverbial monkey wrench into his cranial gears. Von Einsburg's brain was as gooey as a grilled cheese. It marked the end of his Hollywood career, and the beginning of the end for the Indian Alley Gang franchise.

Always something of a mystery, von Einsburg was single, with no known relatives, and so, he became a ward of the state. The judge sent him to an insane asylum north of San Francisco, far from the City of Angels that had driven him mad.

Uncle Bud tried to salvage the Indian Alley Gang. He assigned cameraman Bob MacGyver, my now deceased client, as our new director. But fans could tell the difference. Von Einsburg was the genius behind the series, and that was that. Moviegoers fell out of love with us, and Monarch dropped the series. I was out of work, as was the rest of the gang.

In spite of this dark chapter in my movie career, Mother was still a shrewd manager. We signed on with Invincible Pictures for a series of

Westerns. I got a horse named Zenith, a dog named Philco, and two pearl-handled 45s, a gift from cowboy legend William S. Hart. I was cast as the juvenile sidekick, riding to the rescue whenever the adult hero needed help. Invincible re-branded me. I became "Buster Blade — Wonder Boy of the Westerns."

Hollywood was coming up roses again, that is, until Mother's untimely accident.

"Alex, did you hear me?" Paloma's silky voice brought me back to her yarrow stalks and their sinister warning.

"Yeah, I heard. It's bad news for Buster."

14
Another One Dead

Monday morning. I often wondered what Paloma did between phone calls and paperwork while I was away. Today was the day I found out. I arrived at Confidential Investigations to find my assistant sewing tassels onto a pair of red satin pasties. I have to admit, this was better than watching her count yarrow sticks.

Paloma was the Sky Room's bubble dance understudy. Whenever Ming Toy, the club's regular bubble dancer, couldn't go on, Paloma covered for her. Something that mystified me, though, were the two racks of costumes Paloma kept in the spare room. Fact: all she ever wore on stage was a pair of pasties and a nude thong. What were all those costumes for?

I sidled up to her desk and chirped: "Next thing I know you'll be taking up needle point. What's with the pasties, Peach Blossom?"

She put down her needle and thread.

"My other pair was stolen," she said with righteous indignation. "Sun Lee said it was the club bouncer. He sold them to one of my secret admirers. You know, I think I'll mass produce these things and sell them as intimate

apparel, or maybe even Sky Room souvenirs for sailors to take home and show their buddies. Anyway, these are almost done. What do you think?"

She held them up to her rack, like two fried eggs.

"They look fine, but your sweater's in the way." I imagined her mounded marvels swinging rhythmically to jungle drums on stage.

"Ha ha, so funny, Alex. Get with the program, huh?"

"Okay, any phone calls, checks, winning lottery numbers in the mail today? Did Money God come down the chimney and fill my stocking full of yen?"

"No to all the above," she fizzled, "because you still haven't made a prosperity shrine to Money God,"

"It's on my To Do list, Kitten. All I need is incense. And everything else."

"You did get a call from Mrs. Asquith. She wants to know if there's been any new developments on her missing hubby."

"She needs a psychic, not a detective."

"Well, she's getting impatient, Alex; said she'd drop by this afternoon. I put your mail and today's Chronicle on your desk."

"Thanks. I'll be in my office, detecting."

She gave me a sympathetic look as I shuffled into my inner sanctum. I rifled the top desk drawer for a pack of Chesterfields and dug out a pathetic looking pack with one gasper left. A paper match from the Sky Room Bar brought it to life. I crumpled the empty pack, tossed it into the wastebasket, and settled into my chair to brood.

Cigarette ashes littered the desk blotter like an early snowfall. I shooed them away with an issue of *Amazing Stories*. It was the special Shaver Mystery edition, and it was a pip. The editor had been pushing the Shaver Mystery stories long before the end of the war, and had whipped up considerable controversy among science fiction fans.

The author, a Philly crane operator for Bethlehem Steel named Richard S. Shaver, claimed he found a secret entrance to the inner earth, with an ancient civilization living there. Thus began a series of adventures among a race of underworld mutants. Eventually clawing his way topside, Shaver decided to make hay selling pulp stories about his discoveries, stating the stories were all based on fact, not fiction, and his editor agreed to print them.

Just as amazing, my copy made a useful tool for sweeping ashes off my desk. I dropped the magazine into a drawer, leaned back in my swivel chair, and opened the *Chronicle*. Post-war chaos littered every page.

A Stanford egghead blamed the California drought for the energy shortage. The price of butter, eggs, and milk was skyrocketing. High inflation was expected to continue through 1948. Union bakery workers were still on strike, as were workers at the Fleishmann yeast plant in Oakland. Cannery line crews walked picket lines in front of the Hunt's tomato plant in Hayward. Hell, even toymakers at the Dinky Toy plant were on strike. Herr Hitler may be dead, but his memory lingered on like a bad case of typhoid.

I was ready to swear off newspapers for good when a blurb on page six in the B section stopped me cold.

Former Child Actor Dies in Freak Accident.

Hollywood juvenile actor Charles "Swifty" Taylor, member of the popular silent movie series The Indian Alley Gang, was found dead in his Banning, California home on Thursday, the victim of a freak accident. Riverside coroner Ralph Finley told the Banning Record an autopsy revealed barbiturates in Taylor's blood. "We are not ruling out suicide," Finley said. Taylor lived alone. He leaves four ex-wives and three children. A retrospective of Taylor's Monarch Studios comedies will take place at Banning's Fox Theater on Friday followed by a recollection by Banning's librarian, William Clapper.

My old pal Swifty — dead! That makes two Indian Alley Gang members gone in just six months, not to mention Bob MacGyver, our cameraman.

I looked in the drawer for another Chesterfield, forgetting I'd smoked my last one. Rifling through the desk a second time I found one stuck in a pencil box. I yelped at Paloma through my office door.

"Put the Asquith quail on ice, Legs! I'm taking the Coast Daylight to Los Angeles. I'll be back in a couple of days."

Surprised by this unexpected news, Paloma gasped, "Are you kidding me, Alex? What about the Asquith case? Why L.A.?"

I slapped the newspaper on her desk.

"Look at this!" I said, jabbing my digit at the article.

"This smells like a day-old flounder," I said. "The last time I saw Swifty, we were kicking the Japs off Peleliu Island. One of Tojo's finest was about to plant a bayonet in my back when Swifty shot him.

"Swifty took shrapnel from a Nip mortar shell two days later. That was his ticket back to San Diego. He sent me a letter from the hospital; said he was going to buy land in the desert. I never pegged him as a pill popper like it says in this obit. Tell the Asquith broad I had to powder on important detective business. Be vague. I'll talk to her as soon as I get back."

15
Coast Daylight

An epidemic of sudden death was spreading among former Monarch Studio - extra space before Studio employees. And the way things were shaping up, Tubby and Swifty might not be the last. As a kid, Tubby Manheim was a jerk, but Swifty and I were pals and fellow Marines during the war. I would not let his death be swept under the rug of police paperwork.

I boarded a Sacramento Northern interurban that took me across the Bay Bridge to Oakland. From there I barely caught the Coast Daylight before it steamed out of Oakland's 16th Street Station. The trip was uneventful, and no one recognized me. Few do these days.

Age is a good cover. Child actors rarely keep their adorable looks into adulthood, and for some of us, the transformation can be downright scary. Take Jackie Coogan. He proved that even the cutest, sweetest Hollywood film kid can age into a balding, overweight double for a Hoboken shoe salesman.

On the rare occasion I do get recognized in a bar or on the street, I guarantee the schmuck will try to punch me in the trumpet to prove how tough he is. Next thing he knows, he's mopping the floor with his mustache. Jack Dempsey, the Manassa Mauler, taught me how to box when I was eight years old.

The Daylight stopped to pick up passengers in Santa Barbara before passing through Summerland, Swifty's hometown. Next stop, Ventura. From there the Daylight sped east, through gigantic boulders that loomed on either side of the train. The rocks looked familiar. This was a shooting location for Invincible Pictures' Westerns. It looked exactly as it did when I rode here with Tom Mix.

The blazing sun over Lancaster scorched the Daylight's stainless steel cars as we sped toward Los Angeles.

The last time I walked the marble floors of LA's Union Station I was in combat boots. We Marines were boarding a train bound for San Diego where a ship waited to take us to the South Pacific. Swifty was there, too, rolling cigarettes. He was always rolling gaspers; one for him and one for me. I swore if I made it back home alive, it would be nothing but factory-made cigs for me.

Twenty minutes later, I boarded a local train bound for Palm Springs.

16
Banning, California

Banning's claim to fame was a pioneering spirit and the 10 Highway that ran straight through the heart of town. It's an unassuming destination with a train station to match. Palm Springs is another twenty-five minutes down the line, but you've got to pass through Banning to get there.

I meandered downtown a few blocks to the *Banning Record*. Its cinderblock building was the green color of moldy bread. Inside the cluttered newsroom I found a single reporter typing like a madman on a beat-up Underwood. His brown pants, unbuttoned brown vest, and pinstriped shirt looked like they had been slept in. His sleeves were rolled up to his elbows, and his hat brim bent up like reporters look in B pictures.

A bell jangled over my head as I opened the door. That's when he stopped to take a gander at what stepped in. He swiveled his chair to face me in the door.

"Hi there!" he said with a friendly grin. "What can we do you for?" Journalists use the royal "we" when referring to themselves. He was a chipper sort, even if I did interrupt his deadline.

"I'm an old friend of Swifty Taylor," I said, getting straight to the point. "I read a wire piece in the *San Francisco Chronicle* about his death. It was awful short on detail, so I thought the *Banning Record* might know a few things the big city papers didn't."

His grin got wider.

"You came to the right place, friend. I covered that story, being the only reporter that works here. Normally there are two of us, but we lost one reporter last month when she got married and moved to Pacific Grove. Haven't found a replacement yet. I don't suppose you know how to type?"

"That's something they forgot to teach us in the service," I said.

"Oh, returning soldier, huh? They're all looking for work these days. Just thought I'd ask."

"No harm in asking," I said. "Since you covered Swifty's death you must have seen the coroner's report."

"Sure did."

"And the cause of death was…?"

"Suffocation."

"How's that?"

"It was taffy. Suffocation by taffy."

"Okay, pal, I know I'm not a local, but you don't expect me to…"

The reporter held up his hand to cut me off.

"Listen, friend, I didn't write that coroner's report, but it was suffocation just the same. The coroner said he died in the kitchen, his face covered in goo. The cops figured he'd been popping pills and just sorta keeled over into a big wad of the stuff. Truth is stranger than fiction, you might say. The toxicology report said he had sleeping pills in his system, so there ya go."

That set me off, and the reporter noticed.

"That peeved look on your puss tells me you don't think much of that report, or am I whistling Dixie?"

"You catch on fast," I growled. "I knew Swifty, and I don't buy it. A pill-popping taffy pull smells so bad I can't believe the cops closed the case."

"Here in Banning, everyone's entitled to their opinion, friend."

"Did you know Swifty?"

"No, not really. I met him a couple times. He stayed pretty much to himself on that little farm of his across the tracks. More than likely you'll find a few of his friends at the theater tonight. Maybe they can answer your questions. The Fox is on West Ramsey, or, as the tourists call it, Highway 10."

"Thanks. How do I find Swifty's farm?"

"Head over to South San Gorgonio, cross the railroad tracks then turn left on East Barbour. It's an unpaved road. You'll see a white clapboard house with a picket fence and a small barn. You can't miss it. There's a water tower next to the house."

I thanked him and went back outside. The clatter of his Underwood filled the room as I started down the sidewalk. South San Gorgonio was only a block from here, and the tracks a few blocks more.

Banning proper ended, more or less, at the railroad tracks. There were a handful of small homes scattered across the desert floor, shacks really, and a few farmhouses with small barns. I sprinted across the tracks, barely missing the cowcatcher of a mile-long freight train heading east. The engineer sat on his air horn to show his displeasure with me.

East Barbour was a dusty road in a hot, desert town on the way to somewhere else. Swifty's farmhouse looked like a desert oasis in the setting sun. Shadows were getting longer, so I made haste.

Chickens roosted behind Swifty's picket fence in the hollows they'd scratched into the desert floor. They were waiting for the sunset, and relief from the heat. All was quiet, and the front door was unlocked.

I'd never been here, but it felt familiar. Swifty had turned his home into a kind of museum to his Hollywood past. Framed photos of our youthful heyday hung everywhere. I saw myself in most of them, the pale kid in patched pants, weather-beaten clodhoppers, newsboy cap, and bulky knit sweater.

I saw photos of Thorner von Einsburg in his trademark director's garb — jodhpurs, riding boots, a wide collar shirt with puffy sleeves, and cravat. He held a megaphone to his lips in one photo, as if he were directing a scene. The photo appeared in a 1922 issue of Silver Screen, if I remember right.

Though von Einsburg rarely smiled, he looked almost human in another picture. He was sitting on a park bench with five-year old Swifty balanced on his knee. In another, the gang crowded into the rear window of von Einsburg's Lincoln town car, mugging for the camera.

The photos brought back memories that the war made me forget. They clawed at the inside of my skull like corpses trying to escape their coffins. I shook off the feeling and went to the kitchen, where Swifty had his final scene. A gooey, tan substance covered his Wedgwood stove. It was taffy, and it was everywhere. Unless I'd seen it for myself, I would have thought the cops were nuts.

Thick, sticky goop hung like frozen candle wax off the kitchen table, the stove, the chairs, even from the light fixture on the ceiling. The murder weapon was an electric taffy puller made by the Ajax Candy Company of Chicago, Illinois. It sat on the table where they found Swifty. They found Tubby in his kitchen, too.

I pulled on the machine's metal arms. They were frozen solid from overheating. I flicked the light switch on the kitchen wall. Nothing. A quick check of the fuse box on the back porch revealed a blown fuse covered in more soot than a Tennessee minstrel show. Swifty put a lot of effort into this freak accident. It boggled the mind how he managed it.

Something on the floor caught my eye — a ribbon of Kodak 35mm movie film, about five inches long. I slipped it into my coat pocket. It must be a clue.

Swifty's neighbors were few and far between, so no one noticed when I left through the back door. I aimed my brogans toward town and crossed the railroad tracks, without mishap this time. It had been a long day, and I was hungry.

I saw a hash house near the train station; one of those streetcar diners you see along the 101. This one was called The Choo Chew Café.

The diner was one of LA's iconic Red Line streetcars, with big, round headlamps at either end. Red Line tracks were being torn up and replaced by California's new freeway system. Streetcars like these were a dime a dozen now, and made prefabricated diners. The destination above the diner's windshield said "Hollywood," but Banning was the end of the line for this one. I opened the screen door and stepped inside. It smelled of hamburger grease.

The lunch counter ran along one side of the car, small booths on the other. A burly, bald beefo in a wife beater and saggy trousers peered at me above the kitchen swing doors. He was a boxing fan, if the framed photos of local pugilists hanging above his head meant anything. The thick carpet of hair on his neck and hands more than made up for the lack of it on his bald head.

Wearily, I pulled myself up to the counter and took a load off. Other than the teenage couple whispering sweet nothings in a booth, I was the only customer. Beefo lumbered my way with pad and pencil in hand.

In a voice as deep as J. Paul Getty's pockets he said, "What can I getcha, Bud?"

I gave him my order — a cup of java and the house special: Grandma's Chicken Fried Steak and Eggs.

That's when the hash-slinging hulk began to chat, like bored diner cooks often do.

"On your way to Palm Springs?" His thick eyebrows shot up and down like wooly bears on a hotplate.

"Nope. I'm here for the Swifty Taylor retrospective at the Fox."

"Oh, yeah. That was sad, real sad. He was one of my regulars. He loved my sweet potato fries and cherry pie. He used to talk about the good old days, you know, when he was a big star in silent pictures."

I was in luck — he knew Swifty. I decided to pump him for information.

"We were in the same outfit during the war. I'd love to talk with some of his friends while I'm in town."

"Well, he had friends, but not many," the cook explained. "Kept to his self, mostly. He and Library Bill was pals, though. Bill's the town librarian. Come to think of it, he was in here the other day. Said he'd be at the Fox tonight to talk about Swifty."

He topped up my coffee cup and returned to the kitchen to whip up Grandma's Special.

After banging pots and pans around like he meant business, he returned with a heavy porcelain plate and laid it on the counter. The plate had pictures of cattle brands of the Old West on the rim. I was so hungry even Grandma's Special tasted good. As I finished my hash browns, I uncovered a picture of a Conestoga wagon. Under the chicken fried steak I found a Pony Express rider. I washed down my special with more hot coffee.

"Delicious," I said, "You must be a culinary school graduate."

Beefo seemed amused. "Me? Ha! Uncle Sam taught me all I know. I was an Army cook at the Battle of the Bulge. I kept Patton up to his six shooters in hamburgers."

It was a joke, and he laughed at it himself. I began to probe.

"Did Swifty come in last week?"

"Sure did. He comes in, I mean, used to come in every Tuesday and Friday. Those were his shopping days. He'd sit at the counter, two seats from where you are now. After lunch he'd buy groceries and chicken feed. Let's see, that was a week ago Tuesday. He never made it in last Friday."

"Did he seem okay, I mean, was he upset or anything?" The brawny cook put down his coffee pot, wiped his hands on his apron, and slapped a thoughtful look on his pan.

"He was a little worked up that day, now that you mention it. Kind of excited. He told me he got an invite to a fan convention. He was going to be on a panel with the kids he used to work with, way back when. Well, guess they aren't kids anymore, are they?"

I said, "You got that right, brother. I bet they'd be about as old as I am by now."

He thought about what I said, and took a closer look at me.

"You're probably right about that, mister. Just about your age. Anyway, he skeedaddled before I could give him his change. Said some bigwig was coming by his place with a cameraman to take movies of him for the promotion. The convention was set for the Cow Palace in San Francisco. In any case, I guess he won't be needin' his change now."

The piece of movie film I found on Swifty's kitchen floor confirmed the cook's story about a cameraman. If the cops already knew about Swifty's mystery guests, they were keeping the lid tight.

I gave Beefo a 50¢ tip. He smiled.

"Come back any time, *compadre*. Any time."

I left Beefo thumbing through a ragged boxing magazine and stepped out into the evening air. I felt a sudden chill.

17
The Fox Theater

The desert air had gone from hot to cold by the time I'd reached Banning's Fox Theater. As theaters go, it was nothing like the palatial San Francisco Fox on Market Street. This was a modest two-story edifice made of brick. The marquee had a floral swirl on top. "Fox," blinked on and off in red neon.

Small shops flanked either side of the ticket booth, a smoke shop being one of them. I went inside for a pack of Chesterfields. The bleached blonde waif behind the counter had a wan, bored look on her desert-tanned face. The job was merely a stepping-stone on the road to Hollywood stardom, or so she hoped. She perked up as I neared the counter.

"Hi, handsome. Just passing through, like everybody else?"

"You're very observant," I said. "Yes, just passing through, but with a short stopover."

Her eyes glazed over with tears of desperation. She looked down at her folded hands, then, regaining composure, asked, "Can I help you?"

"Yes, a pack of Chesterfields, please."

She turned to the wall of neatly shelved cigarette packs, stood on her tiptoes to fetch my Chesterfields from the third shelf, and stretched her pair of shapely pins.

"That'll be 25 cents," she said.

As I handed her the two bits, her fingers dallied on my palm as she took it.

"We have plenty of, uhm, Chesterfields," she said. "More than any shop in Banning. We close at eight in case you need another pack."

"Thanks, angel. You're a sweet kid, but don't wait up for me."

Fans were already lined up at the ticket booth outside. I took my place at the end of the line. Ticket in hand, I gave it to the teen cutie standing at the front door. She tore it in half and returned the stub. Her toy soldier's uniform consisted of sharply creased white satin slacks, a blue satin bolero jacket with gold shoulder braids, and a blue grenadier's Shako hat. I met another girl, same age, wearing the same getup at the

inner lobby doors. She snapped on her flashlight and led me to fifth row center, where she aimed her beam at three empty seats.

I edged my way through a line of kneecaps, lowed my seat and was grateful to sit down. As the theater lights dimmed, a woman with a seat as wide as her piano bench, sat down at an upright piano at the rear of the theater. With great gusto, she began belting out an overture of silent movie standards.

The curtain rose, the lights dimmed, and my past began to flicker across the screen. I saw Swifty, Tubby, Biscuits, Carla Darla, Amnesia, Stinky, and Sparky. We were building a taxicab from a derelict car in Swifty's back yard.

We designed an ingenious motor: a dog on a treadmill with a caged cat at the front end. Every kid worth his salt knew the dog would start running as soon as it saw the cat. The dog's treadmill turned the rear wheels and we were off to the races.

The plan was to earn enough money to finance a fishing trip to Camp U Needa Rest. Haycroft, the gang's clubhouse mule, towed the taxi, with us kids inside, up a hill for a test run. The fun began when Biscuits pumped the brakes. Sparky forgot to install them. We gained speed. Along the way, we knocked down a policeman directing traffic. We zoomed through a crosswalk and scared a little old lady who picked up her skirts and ran off in fast motion. We caused mayhem everywhere we went, until we crashed into the duck pond at City Park.

The final offering was *Mother's Little Helper*. Swifty's stage mom, played by Betty Birdseye, put Swifty in charge of Baby Persimmon, his younger brother. I was conspicuously absent from this one, being on loan to Altascope Pictures for a Charlie Chase programmer.

Betty gave Swifty instructions on his brother's care and feeding, and left the house for a PTA meeting. As soon as the front door closed behind her, the gang came rushing in from the backyard. They ran straight to the candy jar, but it was empty. That's when Swifty, always the inventor, came up with a bright idea. He'd whip up a batch of salt water taffy using the family's electric fan to run a makeshift taffy puller. As usual, everything went wrong. Soon the machine was out of control. Taffy flew all over the kitchen.

Peels of laughter racked the audience as the rogue taffy machine began to cover Swifty in thick gobs of goo. I felt my nerve ends going numb. I had either forgotten this picture or had never seen it. Through some bizarre coincidence, it foreshadowed Swifty's mystery death 25 years in the future. As the crowd laughed themselves silly, I sat in stunned disbelief.

The reporter was right. Truth is stranger than fiction.

18
Library Bill

The end of *Mother's Little Helper* brought up the lights, and a man in the front row left his seat and walked up on stage. He introduced himself. William Clapper, better known to locals as Library Bill, was head librarian at the Banning Public Library. He had prepared a short speech about Swifty, he said.

Clapper recalled the first day Swifty came into the library, and how from then on he spent every Thursday afternoon in the periodicals section, pouring over newspapers. Swifty had a regular routine that never varied. I had already heard about this schedule from the cook at The Choo Chew Café. On Tuesdays and Fridays Swifty lunched at the diner, then went shopping at The Food Circus, the local grocery. Thursday was library day. Swifty spent Monday and Wednesday working on his farm. With a few more personal anecdotes and a brief history of Swifty's career at Monarch Studios, Clapper wrapped up his talk. The audience applauded and began filing out, leaving a trail of cigarette butts and popcorn.

As the fans trickled out, I introduced myself to Clapper. He was of medium build, medium height, with wavy brown hair. His tired eyes looked as though they'd read a million books. He had a subdued, librarian's demeanor. I gave him the same line I gave everyone else: I was Swifty's pal, we fought in the war together, and I was hoping to learn more about his life in Banning.

I baited my hook and pointed out the similarity between Swifty's actual death and the scene we'd just witnessed on the big screen.

"Yes, it did strike me as an odd," Clapper said. "A strange coincidence. I didn't know Swifty was such a taffy lover. But, he didn't tell me everything."

I opened the pack of Chesterfields I'd purchased from the blonde waif earlier.

"Swifty and I were close," I said. "I find his death incompatible with what I knew about him. *Mother's Little Helper* makes his death even more puzzling to me. Did you talk to him the week before he died?"

"Yes, a week ago last Thursday at the library," he recalled. "Swifty asked me if the library had a history of the independent movie studios of the 1920s, especially Monarch Studios. I knew he'd worked for Monarch as a kid, so I thought he might be researching his memoir. I had to tell him we didn't have such a book. Then he wrote out a request for a newspaper back issue, and we did have that."

"Do you recall the date and the newspaper?"

"Not off hand, but if you come by the library tomorrow, I'll check the periodicals log and find out."

"Thanks, I'll be there. One more thing: where can I find a decent room for the night?"

"The Del Paso Hotel is just across the street," Clapper said. "It's close and it's clean."

"Thanks. I'll see you tomorrow morning."

19
The Hollywood Detective

The Del Paso Hotel sat on top of a Five and Dime and Hal's Cut Rate Drugs at the corner of West Ramsey and San Gorgonio. The drugstore had fountain service, a rack of the latest magazines, and a selection of big city newspapers. It also had two telephone booths. I slid into one and closed the door. I dialed the office. Right about now Paloma would be collecting her props for tonight's floorshow at the Sky Room. I was right. She picked up.

"Peach Blossom! What's the good word?"

"Alex? Say listen, big boy, I've run out of excuses. Mrs. Asquith wants to know why you're not here tracking down her man."

"Okay, I get it, but I've got a hot lead down here. I'll be back in the office tomorrow afternoon on my honor as a Boy Scout. After my appointment at the Banning library tomorrow morning, I'm outta here."

I wished her luck with the show, and hung up.

I perused Hal's magazine stand. I found a copy of the *Los Angeles Times* and the latest issue of *Dan Turner, Hollywood Detective*. I grabbed both. Hollywood Detective was my favorite mental laxative. It freed up stuck thoughts and got me thinking again. Reading about Dan Turner would make me right as rain, a regular detective. After finding a toothbrush, I paid the clerk and went out into the cool desert air to find a room. The entrance to the hotel was right next door. I walked in.

The Del Paso Hotel featured a California Mission Revival lobby like most Southern California hotels. Its second story windows faced busy West Ramsey, and were shaded from the sun by red canvas awnings.

The clerk at the front desk fluttered to attention as I approached. He gave me the once over.

"Yes, sir?" he warbled cautiously.

"I don't need the Presidential Suite, just something cozy for the night," I said.

"Luggage?"

The question annoyed me.

"Not unless I get some for Christmas."

I flashed a wad of Mrs. Asquith's lettuce. That soothed him. He was an oddly pale denizen in a land so full of sun. Maybe he moonlights at the Banning Mortuary, I thought. A thin, pencil mustache crawled above his upper lip, pulling a twisted smile along with it.

"Of course," the clerk smirked. "That'll be one-fifty. You have Room 17. That's upstairs, and down the hall to your right from the top of the stairs."

He slid the room key across the desk with his left hand. He wore a gold ring on his wedding finger. Some lucky gal.

On my way to the stairs I passed the Phineas Banning Room. A sign on the French doors said breakfast was served beginning at seven AM. I peeked in and counted a dozen tables with white tablecloths. It smelled of pancakes and mesquite, which would have piqued my appetite if I hadn't already stuffed myself at the Choo Chew Cafe.

I made for the communal bathroom down the hall to wash off a few pounds of desert sand. After a quick shower I felt almost human, which for me is really something. Back in my room I stripped down to my skivvies and hopped into the sack to snap on the reading light. I was ready for *Hollywood Detective*. My eyelids got heavy after reading only one Dan Turner yarn, so I turned out the light and sank into the pillow, but I just couldn't stop thinking about *Mother's Little Helper*.

20
Curiouser and Curiouser

The sun rose like a headache to the steady roar of motorcars heading east to Palm Springs. It sounded like a goddamn migration! But these weren't Okies on their way to pick peaches. They were California tourists, making up for years of wartime gas and tire rationing. Now it was full speed ahead and bumper-to-bumper.

A Pacific Greyhound bus ground second gear as it passed under my window. That got my attention. I checked my tank watch. It was seven o'clock, still plenty of time for breakfast in the Phineas Banning Room. I was dressed, teeth brushed, and seated at the breakfast table by eight o'clock. I brought my copy of yesterday's *Los Angeles Times* for a leisurely read.

After two cups of joe, two eggs over easy, four blueberry pancakes, and a second Chesterfield, I was ready for a stroll to the Banning Public Library.

It was a short walk. The library was only two blocks from the hotel. The address Library Bill had given me was for Banning High School. Apparently, Banning couldn't afford a real library, so the city fathers set aside a few rooms at the high school. Bill was waiting for me behind an antique desk that looked like the Pilgrims tossed it overboard before dropping anchor at Plymouth Rock.

We exchanged pleasantries about the weather, and how smog from the new freeway system was cluttering up the fresh, desert air of Banning. Bill beckoned me to the reference desk. He'd already done my homework for me, he said.

"It didn't take long to find Swifty's final periodicals request," Bill said. "It was only a couple weeks ago."

Clapper dropped a heavily bound volume of back issues on the counter. He'd bookmarked it for me.

"This is what Swifty asked for: the morning edition of the *Los Angeles Times* for April 4, 1947."

I wondered what could have happened six months ago that would pique Swifty's interest.

"I have to admit," the librarian confessed, "Thursdays won't be the same here without Swifty. He'd taken a keen interest in Banning history. He even bought a copy of my book, *Banning: Then, Now, and Maybe Later.* He asked me to autograph it for him, and I had him autograph my copy. I know that must sound odd, autographing my own book like that."

I opened the hefty tome to the bookmark on April 4, 1947, scanning slowly, page by page, hoping for a hit. Sure enough, I got one. Someone had cut a hole on page 3 in the B section, probably with a pocketknife. I showed it to Library Bill, whose face sagged down to his naval when he saw it.

I pushed the large volume back to the helpful librarian after jotting down the issue and page number.

"You've been a great help, Bill," I said. "All I need is another copy of this newspaper and I'll know what Swifty wanted. I'll try the San Francisco Library when I get home. By the way, did Swifty say anything to you about a convention he planned to attend in Frisco?"

"Now that you mention it, he did. He'd gotten a call from a convention staffer who was sending over a cameraman to take a promotional film of some sort. But that's all he said about it."

I thanked Library Bill and boarded the next train to Union Station. Sure, I was using the Asquith broad's dough to investigate Bob MacGyver's case, but I really did it for Swifty. In a few more days I'd locate Asquith's missing bookworm and get her off my neck.

21
The Trouble with Clients

Iris Asquith was picking obsessively at her lace collar in the waiting room when I ankled through the door. The old doll's face had an apoplectic red glow that told me I was about to get an earful. She didn't waste time giving it to me.

"I expected far better results than this, Mr. Blade," she rasped, wiping spittle from her lower lip. "It appears Onslow is of little concern to you."

Without a word, I went to the other room to fetch her husband's luggage. I set it down next to the boiling battle-axe.

"I retrieved Onslow's suitcase from the Hotel Ebner," I grumbled, "and I took the liberty of checking it for clues to his whereabouts. Other than this Southern Pacific train schedule, there weren't any. Someone circled the 7AM train for Santa Cruz, here." I pointed to the aforementioned time noted in the brochure.

"You're saying Onslow took the train to Santa Cruz? Why would he do that?"

"I'm not saying that at all, Mrs. Asquith. We can't even be sure he boarded the train. By the way, did you know your husband withdrew a thousand dollars from his savings account the day he left for Sacramento?"

"I haven't seen this month's bank statement, so I wouldn't know."

"Do you have any idea why he would need that kind of cash? It couldn't have been for his hotel room. The Ebner is a dive."

She shifted uncomfortably in her chair.

"He often buys books from people who want to sell their collections. They often attend the convention for that purpose. Onslow offers them cash, hoping for a better price."

"Considering he picked up this train schedule," I parried, "he could have used it as traveling money. A man can go a long way on a thousand dollars. Does your husband have any friends or relatives he might stay with?"

"No, he has no living relatives. The only people he saw on a regular basis were his customers. He had many of those."

I was getting nowhere fast, so I changed gears.

"By the way, I learned that you and your husband were in a vaudeville act together. He was Mandark, Supreme Master of Magic, and you were his assistant. It must have been an interesting time."

"Yes, it was. But that has nothing to do with Onslow's disappearance."

"Why do you say that, Mrs. Asquith?"

"Because it was a long time ago, long before we moved to California."

"I'm curious, why did you choose San Francisco?"

"Onslow felt it was the kind of town that would support a metaphysical book store. Besides, San Francisco seemed a long way off from the Dearborn mess. We blended into the scenery here."

It could have been the truth. Frisco was a sure bet for Onslow's taste in reading material. It's a hotbed of Theosophists, spiritualists, astrologers, vegans, and flying saucer buffs hoping for a one-way ticket to Venus.

After convincing the Asquith pain-in-the-neck I was on the verge of a big break in the case, I escorted her down the hall to the stairs. I wasn't on the verge of anything, but that got rid of her.

I should have felt like a heel for fibbing, but in this case, not so much.

22
The Flying Fish

With Iris Asquith out of the way, I sifted through the day's mail. Under a few past due notices I uncovered a package wrapped in brown paper, tied with string. The handwriting in the left-hand corner read, "Charles Taylor, Banning, California." It was from Swifty!

I cut the string with my Indian Alley Gang souvenir pocketknife and ripped it open. A news clipping fell onto the desktop. Right away I recognized it — the purloined piece from Library Bill's newspaper! I unwrapped further and found a scrapbook, the kind sold in five and dimes. The embossed fake leather cover read, "Banning, California." Under that, a hook-nosed Indian chief sat cross-legged next to a teepee.

Pasted to each of the scrapbook's heavy, black pages were clippings about the Indian Alley Gang, the history of our Hollywood career. One was about the time we appeared at the Million Dollar Theater in downtown Los Angeles. Another showed the Gang cavorting in the Neptune pool at William Randolph Hearst's San Simeon estate. I flipped through a few more pages and found ads for Indian Alley Gang toys, breakfast cereals, dolls, candy, books, clothing, and pocketknives, like the one I used to open this package.

Swifty had saved magazine features too. In the days when we were Hollywood stars our fans wanted to know everything about us, like our favorite ice cream, whether we owned a pet and what its name was; what did our parents imagine for us when we were grown up? Monarch doled out the standard PR line about how our moms and dads set aside trust funds for our college educations.

It sounded good, but it was as phony as Harry Truman's Loyalty Oath. Monarch Studios came up with one whopper after another, making our parents sound like caring adults. Truth be told, they were in love with their Hollywood lifestyle. None of the Gang ever saw a penny of what they'd earned from the galloping snapshots, and that included me.

Turning another page I found a story cut from a 1924 *Movie News* about Thorner von Einsburg's nervous breakdown. After the studio shelved *Baby Bwana*, von Einsburg moved to Napa State Hospital insane asylum, the final chapter of his film career.

I paid extra attention to the clipping Swifty swiped from the Banning library.

April 4, 1947

Santa Catalina, California

Former child star Chatsworth "Sparky" McFadden died last week in an apparent boating accident while fishing off Catalina. An Avalon resident walking his dog on Descanso Beach discovered McFadden's body and notified sheriff's deputies. McFadden's boat, the Flying Fish, was later found adrift near Two Harbors.

Fellow Indian Alley Gang member Luther 'Biscuits' Brown, now an ordained minister who goes by the name "Peace It's Wonderful" Brown, said in a telephone interview that, "Sparky's old gang and his many fans will sorely miss him. He has gone to heaven to take his place among the stars on the Lord's silver screen."

McFadden was a board member of the Foundation for Child Screen Actors (FCSA), which helps child actors "...make the transition from Hollywood juvenile actor to the workaday world of adulthood," according to its mission statement. A burial at sea off Catalina Island is planned for next Monday.

That made three: Tubby, Swifty, and now Sparky. No, make it four. I forgot MacGyver.

Why the law had not connected these so-called accidental deaths was beyond me. Swifty knew something was going on, and so did MacGyver. Maybe small-town law enforcement, with its lack of know-how and manpower, had no time for in-depth investigations. In any case, no one was paying attention, including news reporters. Even St. James hadn't noticed the connection yet. I could have let him in on it, but his low opinion of my chosen career made me lose interest.

Hell, until MacGyver came along, I might have overlooked Tubby's demise too. And Swifty died right after he mailed this clipping about Sparky. Maybe Paloma's yarrow sticks were right: maybe I'm being fitted for a wooden overcoat.

I turned over Sparky's obit. A piece of masking tape stuck to the back had two words written in pencil: *Flying Fish*!! Swifty underlined it, adding urgency to his exclamation points. The obit mentioned Sparky's boat named *Flying Fish*. Nothing unusual about that. Anyone who's been to Catalina knows that flying fish are a big tourist attraction

there. Whole schools of the little sea bats take to the air every summer. Boatloads of Kodak-wielding tourists love to take snapshots of them.

On the other hand, *Flying Fish* was also the title of a 1924 Indian Alley Gang short. That was the year Monarch Studios chartered a white steamer to take the gang and its film crew to Catalina. I hadn't seen that picture in years, but I recalled the final scene had Sparky and Biscuits fishing off the pier in Avalon Bay.

Sparky hooked a flying fish that zoomed skyward like a Nazi V2 rocket. After a hair-raising flight over Avalon with Sparky in tow, the fish dove back into the bay. Meanwhile, Biscuits saw that Sparky was in big trouble. So, Biscuits used his fishing pole to hook the seat of Sparky's pants and reel him out of the drink. *Flying Fish* was one of Monarch Studio's most popular Indian Alley Gang productions.

Why was I being pulled back to a time I hadn't thought about in years?

23
Disaster Strikes

You might say kid actors never recover from life as a celluloid commodity. We were stocks and bonds in short pants, and maybe that's why every member of the gang had a fair share of problems. I was no exception.

In 1916, the year I was born, Mother moved from Albuquerque, New Mexico to California. She craved the kind of excitement Hollywood had to offer, and as soon as we dropped anchor in Pasadena, she got a job as an extra on D.W. Griffith's epic, *Birth of a Nation*.

Griffith had a huge budget, the biggest in Tinsel Town, and he needed extras, plenty of them. They cast Mother as a plantation owner's wife molested by former slaves, all played by white actors in black face.

That's when Mother met her future boyfriend, Carl Dietrich. Dietrich played a Klansman on horseback. Carl, or *Uncle* Carl as Mother asked me to call him, was a rodeo cowboy who came to Hollywood looking for work as a horse trainer and stunt rider. It didn't take long before *Uncle* Carl began lounging around our Pasadena bungalow.

Mother and Carl must have watched *Birth of a Nation* a dozen times in nearly that many theaters across LA. Mother was a huge Griffith fan. She thought he was a genius. The film was a hit in its day, but it was free advertising for the Ku Klux Klan, and the Klan took full advantage of its new notoriety by sending its minions out west for a membership drive. When they got to Hollywood, Mother and Carl signed up.

Carl began to climb the organizational ladder. For a time he was Grand Cyclops of the Orange County klavern, and he was still climbing. He and Mother attended their meetings every month, not including the parades, cross burnings, and lord knows what else.

After signing with Monarch Studios, we moved out of the Morengo bungalow into higher class digs in the neighboring village of San Marino. We lived three houses away from Earl Derr Biggers' two-story hacienda. Finally, we had arrived.

As often happens in Hollywood, careers vanish overnight. The end of mine came one weekend in September. I never did enjoy boring Klan gatherings, so Mother would ask the neighbor lady next door to keep an eye on me whenever she and Carl went out on Klan night. One of those nights they left for a rally in Anaheim, to be followed by a parade through town.

Carl imbibed heavily during Klan activities, despite Mother's protests. By the time they left Anaheim that evening, Carl was sloshed. Rounding a curve on the 101, he drove Mother's Packard Clipper through a guardrail. They died in their bloodstained robes.

Mother left no will and had no estate. The bottom line was, Mother and *Uncle* Carl had squandered my showbiz fortune on lavish parties, a mortgaged home in San Marino, and donations to the Klan. I was 11 years old and broke. It was an old Hollywood story, and it happened to the biggest and best, like Jackie Cooper, Baby Peggy, even Jackie Coogan. Hell, these days, Alfalfa tends bar in Santa Monica to make ends meet.

After the accident, Swifty's family in San Gabriel took me in until Uncle Jesse could drive down from Frisco to pick me up. He and Aunt Maida raised me like their own. Uncle Jesse told me about the time Carl snuck into our Pasadena home dressed in his Klan robes to scare the bejeezus out of me. That explained my nightmares, but it didn't stop them.

I've known battle-fatigued soldiers who developed neuroses during the war, but I got mine right here in Hollywood, California. In fact, I never knew a Hollywood brat who wasn't up to his neck in therapists. I was lucky enough to find Dr. Ivan Ching right here in Chinatown.

24
Dr. I. Ching

Dr. Ching's ad in the Chinese Yellow Pages billed him as an "Herbalist and Attitude Adjustment Counselor." If he was a doctor, I'm not aware of what kind he was. He kept a tiny, two-room office on Waverly Place. His suite was sandwiched between the Tin How Temple above, and a tong headquarters masquerading as a Chinese music society below.

In both Chinese and English the sign on his office door read: "I. Ching — Confucius Wisdom Solve All Your Problems." Besides mental stability, I. Ching sold Chinese lottery tickets and exotic elixirs made of ground rhino horn and powdered tiger's penis.

To keep overhead low, Ching arranged his therapy couch behind a bamboo screen inside the herb shop. It didn't offer much privacy, but privacy was a rare commodity in Chinatown. Every third Friday I lounged on Ching's lumpy horsehair couch, watching him puff serenely on an herbal cigarette. He began each session exactly the same way:

"What brings honorable detective to I. Ching's humble temple of serenity?"

"Big trouble, Mr. Ching," I began. "Three fellow actors from my Hollywood past have all died in mysterious ways. There's got to be a reason, but I can't see what it is. The cops say the deaths were accidental, but they're a bunch of dopes."

After a few thoughtful drags on his Oriental coffin nail, the shaman replied, "When player cannot see man who deal cards, much wiser to stay out of game."

"I hear you, doc, but that's not how this business works. And Swifty Taylor was one of the deceased. He saved my life during the war. I owe it to Swifty to find out what happened to him."

Mr. Ching could be stubborn. He was starting to dig in his heels. Poised on his bamboo throne, cigarette in hand, he reminded me of the caterpillar from Alice in Wonderland.

"Foolish is rooster who stick head in lawn mower," he warned. "End up in stew."

"Are you saying I should drop the case?"

"Man who seek trouble, never find it far off," he replied.

"That's what my secretary says."

"Woman's voice like monastery bell," Ching pontificated. "When tolling, must attend."

"Look, Dr. Ching, all I want to know is where can I dig up a solid lead on Swifty's death."

My persistence seemed to annoy Ching. A few more puffs, and his mood finally lifted.

"Good detective look for something unusual," he advised. "Okay, time up. That will be two dollars."

Ching was a bargain if nothing else. I left his therapeutic tea palace and began the slow climb back to the Mayfair Building. Paloma was in the office when I arrived.

"Hi, Legs. Any new complaints from the Asquith bat?"

"Not in the last 24 minutes. Say, you forgot to leave a contact number with me when you left this morning. You know how I..." She stopped in mid sentence.

"Ohhhh, that's right. I nearly forgot," she said. "It's the third Friday of the month."

"You are correct, kitten."

"That means you're still seeing that shyster Ching, huh? You do realize he gets this so-called wisdom from watching Charlie Chan movies. You know that, right? I hate to say it, Alex, but people of the white persuasion fall for his shtick every time."

"Say what you will about Dr. Ching, Paloma, but he's given me some pretty good advice."

"Are you serious?" Paloma berated. "Those clichés of his are like ink blots. They mean whatever you want them to mean."

"Okay, what do you expect? I grew up in Hollywood. I can't kick the Chan habit."

"Try harder."

"It might interest you to know, peach blossom, that you and Ching are on the same page concerning the mystery deaths. He advised me to back off. I told him no way."

"And what did he say to that?"

"Smart detective look for something unusual."

"Oh, that explains everything. If you really want to see something unusual, Alex, go look in the mirror."

If there's one thing I've learned from Paloma, never argue with a Spanish-Chinese babe. You'll never win. I decided to let the bee in her bonnet buzz a while without me.

"I'll meditate on that, Legs," I said cheerily. "Meanwhile, I'd better check Red's Place for messages. I'll be back in a jiff."

25
Television

Two hours later, I returned to the office to find Paloma sitting in the dark, watching television. As per our office agreement, she'd requested a TV set to entertain waiting clients, but I knew who really wanted it. For one thing, TV programming doesn't start until after business hours. Nevertheless, I got a monthly installment plan from Chung's Radio-TV on Grant. They put an antenna on the roof.

I was standing three feet away; Paloma didn't see or hear me. She was too busy watching "Let's Rumba," a dance instruction show. What baloney.

"How can you watch that crap, Legs? What's the big deal with television anyway? It's a fad, like shoulder pads and long skirts. Nothing's gonna replace Fibber Magee and Molly on the radio."

"For one thing," Paloma shot back, "you can improve yourself by watching television. Take this show. I'm learning how to rumba. Get with the times, grandpa. Radio is out. Pretty soon every apartment in Chinatown will have a television set. Bookstores will be a thing of the past, and so will your pulp magazines. Television is big, Alex, really big."

"Yeah, sure. The rumba will make me an Einstein. I'm telling you, Legs, the only good thing about television is radio."

"Ten years from now you'll still be wearing celluloid shirt collars, Alex."

"And I don't believe in frozen food, or whipped cream that comes out of spray cans, either," I yapped.

Then it hit me like a piano falling from a third story window. Paloma should have been getting ready for her gig at the Sky Room. Instead, she was decked out in a red Betty Levay dress and black nylons. She was dressed for good luck, Chinese style. I was mildly perplexed.

"Shouldn't you be getting ready for the show tonight, Legs?"

Paloma frowned. "It's my night off. You're taking me to the Black Cat to see *La Vie Bohemiénne*. Or did you forget?"

I did, but I better not let her know that.

"No way," I fibbed. "Your dreamy good looks just stunned me, that's all. Let's grab a bite at Buon Gusto in North Beach. After that, we'll go to the Black Cat and be there in plenty of time for the play."

The Black Cat was Paloma's favorite hangout, an offbeat coffeehouse at the edge of North Beach just off Columbus. Intellectuals from Frisco's Little Bohemia read poetry and critique manifestoes at The Black Cat. It was a magnet for the city's poets, artists, nudists, and First Amendment activists. You can order Italian espresso, strong and black, made on a fancy chrome steamer that came all the way from Milan, Italy.

We'd barely set foot in Gommorah when a couple of hedonists near the front door glued their eye sockets on Paloma. They began sweating copious amounts of hormones at the sight of her. I moved them aside and took us to a table next to a potted plant with a sign drooping on a withered limb. "Free Speech Zone," it said.

The scent of incense and reefer wafted through a back-room door. A stage made of two-by-fours and plywood sat empty against a bare brick wall. I assumed this was where *La Vie Bohemiénne* would unfold.

Each small table came equipped with two folding chairs and an empty Chianti bottle with a lit candle stuck in its neck. Layers and layers of red, white, and green wax had melted down the bottles. The chairs were as comfy as mousetraps, but the other patrons didn't seem to care. They were too busy nursing cappuccinos and scribbling important thoughts on large yellow notepads.

I squirmed on my rickety seat. "What's this play about, Moon Cakes?"

"It has to do with the Communist witch hunt going on in Hollywood," Paloma replied, "and the oppression of artists and intellectuals in the name of so-called patriotism."

"Oh, a political passion play, huh? Do they serve alcohol here?"

"No, they don't. Just keep an open mind, okay, Alex? You might learn something new."

"I learned something new about television today. No more Fibber McGee."

I felt a tap on my shoulder. I swiveled around and lamped Stan Raycraft, ace reporter for the *Call-Bulletin* standing behind me with a well-known goofy grin.

Stan was a couple inches shorter than my six three. He had a sturdy build and dark brown hair swept back in a shiny pomp. His wire frame specs gave him the look of a scholar, and his crumpled clothing and lack of a necktie hinted at the Tenderloin flophouse where he lived.

Stan was a sharp cookie. His investigative reporting had exposed the Bay Area's wartime black market. It ruffled plenty of feathers, and he stepped on a lot of fat cats' toes along the way. That put pressure on his publisher. After that, Stan's beat changed as often as a baby's diaper. His editor assigned Stan nothing but puff pieces after that.

Tonight, Stan had an eager look on his mug.

"Hey, Alex, hi, Paloma! Mind if I join you?"

"If you can find a chair, bring it over," I said. He borrowed one from a bearded artist sketching portraits in charcoal.

"Don't tell me your editor's got you on the arts and entertainment beat," I laughed.

"Indeed he has, Big Daddy. My review of *La Vie Bohemiénne* will appear in the theater section of the Sunday edition. It is verboten that I should cover stories with controversial subject matter, like invasions from outer space and crooked politicians. So, I get arts and entertainment. But that's not why I want to talk to you, Buster. Have you heard about Swifty Taylor?"

"Yeah, I heard."

"And you've also heard about Sparky McFadden's drowning off Catalina?"

"Sparky did love to go fishing on his days off," I evaded.

"And what about Tubby Manheim? If I were a betting man, and you know I am, I'd say you've got the inside track to Obitsville, Daddy-o."

"Are you just trying to scare me, Stan, or is this a fishing trip?"

"You know me, Alex. I can smell a story with one nostril tied behind my back. These goofball deaths have got to be on your radar, right? I just don't want anything to happen to you — unless I'm there to cover it."

"Thanks, it's nice to know you're looking out for me. But the cops don't agree. Accidental death is the way they see it."

"Gimme a break!" Stan said, working himself into a snit. "Those hick town police departments don't have the manpower or the brain power to handle cases like these. I can't believe you'd go along with that. These deaths were most unusual!"

Stan was wound up like a street corner preacher.

"And what about MacGyver?" he raved on. "I heard about his murder over the police radio band after you called it in. I got curious, so I looked him up. He worked at Monarch Studios the same time you did. What're the odds of that? In case you didn't know, the homicide squad is at an impasse on the MacGyver case, and St. James is pissed."

I shrugged. "When isn't he pissed? I'm just trying to scratch out a living here, Stan."

He turned to Paloma with pleading eyes.

"Can you talk some sense into this goofball, beautiful?"

Paloma put her hand on my arm and squeezed. "Stan's right, Alex. Why don't you let him in on this one? Maybe he can help."

The conversation ended when the house lights flashed, signaling the play was about to begin.

All attention focused on the stage where two men and a woman were engaged in a mock trial. The men sat on stools behind a crudely painted plywood bench. They wore black robes like English magistrates. Their long, white wigs drooped over their shoulders.

A cute blonde bimbo of about 20 stood in the docket, which amounted to a railing made of two-by-fours nailed together.

Blondie wore a bulky green sweater with oversized turtleneck. The sweater did nothing for my imagination, but under that, her black tights outlined a pair of shapely pins. Other than her lipstick, which was fire engine red, she wore no makeup.

As the audience got quiet, a judge banged his gavel.

"Miss Andrea Kominski," the judge said with plenty of ham, "as a Hollywood screenwriter you are charged with the treasonous act of aiding and abetting the enemy by disseminating Stalin's Communist agenda to unsuspecting Americans throughout this great land. How do you plead?"

This was the blonde wren's cue. But instead of entering a plea, she began to disrobe. This was her act of defiance to authoritarianism. Ever so slowly her fingers rolled the black tights down her luscious legs. This exposed an expanse of ivory epidermis and diaphanous silk step-ins. She then turned her attention to the shapeless tent that doubled as her sweater.

She pulled it up and over her head with both hands. The sweater hit the floor. She was all slim curves and contours. By now the audience was whooping and waving their flippers in the air like a bunch of hungry sea lions.

Blondie turned to face the brick wall for her *coup de gras*. She reached behind her back, unsnapped her brassiere and let gravity take over. She spun around. That revealed a pair of pink torpedoes that would have sunk the Bismarck. As she was about to lower her step-ins to half-mast, the SFPD came pouring through the front door like a swarm of termites.

One of the blue gorillas growled, "This is a raid, keep your seats!"

A harness bull stood guard at every portal. I turned and grinned at Stan.

"Looks like this'll be a short review, Stanley."

The cops cuffed the actors and threw a coat over Miss Kominski. They also arrested the bartender, who had sapped a swabbie during a brawl at last night's performance of this same play. The sailor turned out to be Miss Kominski's boyfriend. Long story short, fists began to fly when Popeye saw Olive Oil frolicking in the buff in front of Bluto. When the swabbie woke up from his nap, he filed an assault charge on the bartender.

That was all the fuzz needed to raid The Black Cat, a known den of Socialists and avid readers. The officer in charge walked on the stage announced:

"Peep show's over, people! Go home and be thankful we didn't haul you in too!"

Stan edged up to my ear so I could hear him over the din.

"Don't forget, Alex, I want in on your case. I can help you with legwork, anything you need. You're my ticket out of the arts and entertainment beat. I need greener pastures. Here's my phone number. Call me, man!"

I cupped my hands and yelled back, "Come by the office Monday morning after nine."

Stan turned on his grin. "Solid, Daddy-o!"

Paloma snagged my arm and we filed out of The Black Cat with the rest of the Bohemians.

26
Stan Raycraft

Chinatown was a smoldering ruin after the 1906 earthquake, but that had an unexpected outcome. It transformed Chinatown into what it is today—an Oriental fantasy made for the tourist trade. A group of Chinese businessmen hired two Anglo architects to design buildings with an exotic, foreign look. They added sweeping pagoda roofs with red and green tiles, filigree balconies, street lamps that resembled Chinese lanterns, and narrow alleys that filled up with gambling dens and the scent of sandalwood. It was the next best thing to a Hollywood movie set, and its Chinese residents were its unpaid extras. They brought realism to an otherwise imaginary scene.

I was on my way to the Photo Den, a portrait studio crammed among the bazaars and tearooms on the 400 block of Grant Avenue. "Photos developed while you wait," according to the sign board out front.

The Photo Den specialized in gag photos for tourists, with a selection of cartoon bodies painted on plywood with oval cutouts to stick your face into. Among the portraits offered were weightlifters, hula dancers, old time sailors, boxers, a man in the moon, a man pulling a rickshaw, and a Mandarin potentate decked out on a throne. It was the go-to place for servicemen to have their picture taken in Chinatown.

My contact, Betty Lam, worked the day shift there. She also took head shots for entertainers, and even moonlighted as a crime photographer by night. She had the dirt on all the show biz types passing through town. She was arranging three servicemen for a group portrait when I stepped through the door.

She wore a Chinese embroidered red silk gown with gold trim, and a red silk hat with tassels dangling from the brim. This impressed the tourists, who craved to see "authentic" Chinese here, like they'd seen in Hollywood movies.

Betty took the shot, pulled the film holder out of her Crown Graphic, and gave it to her assistant to develop. That was my cue to sidle up to her.

"What's cookin' good lookin'?" I yodeled.

"Why, Buster Blade! Long time no see. I hear you got your PI's license. Now you really mean business, huh?"

"I'll bet you also heard I set up shop in the Mayfair Building, on the Occidental side of Stockton."

"Yeah, Paloma told me about that. She came in for a sitting last week. She brought her bubble, too. I got a great shot. It shows just enough skin while maintaining family sensibility."

"Yeah, Paloma's a busy girl," I said. "Say, Betty, can I pick your brain? I'm looking for dope on an old-time vaudeville act. Mandark, Supreme Master of Magic. Ever heard of him?"

"*Vaudeville*? Do I look that old, Alex?" Betty made a sad face followed by a big smile. "I've seen plenty of acts, but that one's before my time. I'll tell you who might know; Willy Wang. He owns the Dragon's Lair. He's been around Chinatown forever. You know, Old Country Chinese who made good? He was booking acts years before the clubs came to Chinatown. Mr. Wang and Mr. Ching are big wigs in the same tong — excuse me — benevolent society. Say, are you still seeing that Shanghai shyster Ching?"

Before I opened my yap, a family with a Midwest air about them wandered in. Dad gave the den a look-see. An Argus camera hung around his neck. He told Betty he wanted a portrait of the little woman and his kids in front of the painted Chinese pagoda with "Greetings from Chinatown" printed on the picture. I thanked Betty and got out of there before she gave me any grief about Dr. Ching.

27
Portsmouth Square

The Dragon's Lair was a subterranean thirst emporium with an all-Chinese glamour girl review. It faced Portsmouth Square, Chinatown's communal living room. The Spaniards built the square when they founded San Francisco, but the Mexicans replaced them after the revolution. The gringos replaced the Mexicans in 1846. Finally, the Chinese claimed Portsmouth Square without firing a shot, and they're still here. They sit around their makeshift tables playing cards seven days a week. It's a big social scene.

The Dragon's Lair was open for business, but it was too early for the floorshow, "Naked Chinatown." I approached the bar, tended by a swarthy Latin type with curly dark hair. He looked Italian, dressed casual. I saw in his eyes he sized me up as a cop.

"I'd like to see Mr. Wang. The name is Alexander Blade."

"What's the beef?"

"No beef. Betty Lam sent me. She said Mr. Wang might know about a vaudeville act I'm researching."

He flicked a switch behind the bar and leaned down.

"A gentleman here says he wants to see you about a vaudeville act, Mr. Wang."

A thin, high-pitched voice crackled over a hidden speaker behind the bar. The voice could have been a child's. A buzzer buzzed in the door behind me. I opened it and faced a dimly lit corridor.

"Mr. Wang's office is at the far end of the hall," the bartender said. "Follow the red carpet to his office and knock on the door that says 'Mr. Wang.' As long as you stay on the carpet, you can't miss."

I stepped into the corridor and the door closed behind me. The floor felt like I was walking downhill. It must have been an old-time speakeasy during Prohibition.

The corridor ended in a dimly lit cellar with brick walls. It smelled of damp earth, like an open grave. Six tall Chinese vases, their fluted mouths at eye level, flanked the red carpet on either side of the room. Just beyond the vases I saw a flight of stairs that continued down. At the bottom of the stairs, two life-sized ceramic lions crouched on either side of an ancient pair of black lacquered doors. The doors had gold Chinese characters painted on them, but the paint had worn off in parts.

I pushed open the doors and entered a cavernous room. Call me crazy, but I was looking at the bow of a wooden sailing ship. And it wasn't just the bow, it was the entire ship! The name, *Niantic*, was barely legible on the bow.

Someone had cut a door into the starboard side of the ship, where the red carpet made a sharp turn and continued inside. Painted above the door in freehand lettering I saw, "Rest for the weary and storage for trunks." I was looking at a 19th Century whaling ship turned Gold Rush hotel! The ship's masts, as thick as telephone poles, rose into the upper floor. Electric light bulbs hanging from the upper beams cast a yellow glow on my surroundings.

I had heard of such ships. They were an urban legend among the city's old timers. Frisco became a burial ground for these wooden ships during the Gold Rush. Desperate to reach the gold fields, entire crews jumped ship after dropping anchor in the bay. Within months, San Francisco's shoreline was littered with scores of abandoned ships.

As gold flowed into the city it began growing at a fantastic pace. Everything was in short supply, especially building materials. That's when enterprising citizens began hauling the abandoned ships ashore, converting them into hotels, brothels, shops, even jails.

Frisco's original shoreline gradually disappeared, filled in with rocks, dirt, and wooden ships run aground. The ships were buried and forgotten. The *Niantic* was one of those buried ships, left for dead on the shores of Portsmouth Square a century ago.

A flight of stairs led from the hold to the upper deck, where I saw a pair of weathered doors with a brass plate. "Mr. Wang," it said. I knocked. The falsetto voice I'd heard at the bar said, "Come in, pleeese!"

Willie Wang's cadaverous face watched me from behind a black lacquered desk. Several paper lanterns hung from the cabin ceiling.

A golden statue of the laughing Buddha reclined with an offering of incense, oranges, and Chinese pastries. Smoke from the incense drifted to the ceiling, made a U turn, and fell back down to the floor where it collected in writhing heaps. The heavy fragrance added to the room's earthy feel.

The ghostly face said, "How can Mr. Wang help honorable gentleman today?"

He was old school Chinese, all right, just like Betty said he was, complete with Dr. Ching's pidgin English. The accent was what Wang's white patrons expected to hear when they came to Chinatown.

The frail man was thriftily attired in a single-breasted Trentwood Deluxe from Sears. His hand-painted silk tie had egrets in flight. He wore his thinning white hair pulled back in a short ponytail, and three fingers on each of his hands had gold rings. The rings flashed when they caught light from the lanterns.

"I'm Alexander Blade, Mr. Wang, a private investigator working on a case. I'm looking for information on a vaudeville act from 30 years ago. Betty Lam said if a theatrical act ever came through town, you'd know about it. Is that right?"

"This may be so," Wang said in a voice like fingernails on a chalkboard. "I am knowing many an entertainer. I am eighty-five year young. Know many people, yes."

He glanced at the spent joss sticks on his altar, reached into a desk drawer and pulled out a bundle of yellow incense wrapped in red twine. He lit a dozen sticks with a gold lighter and stuck them into a bowl of sand on the altar. He looked satisfied, so I continued.

"Have you ever heard of a magician by the name of Mandark, Supreme Master of Magic?"

"So so so! Mandark? He long time ago. Not know what he do now. I book him at Orpheum, two, maybe three time. No, maybe two at Orpheum, one for Sutro. He want to star in *dianyang*. You know, the moving picture."

"Yes, that's him. Then you must have seen his act?"

"Very good act. Yes, very unusual. He bill himself, Man Who Travel Through Time and Space. He disappear on stage, and come back on balcony, on street, on roof, in other buildings. Big surprise to audience. Beautiful assistant also his girlfriend. Forget name, Tulip? Like flower. They marry much later."

He summed up, "Not much else Mr. Wang know about Mandark."

"Do you recall the last time you booked their act?"

"Oh, long time. Want to say, uh, 1918. But do not quote Mr. Wang on that. Memory like good liar, often distort fact."

I thanked Wang and followed the red carpet out of the *Niantic*, through the long corridor, back to Grant Avenue where I filled my lungs with fresh air. My next stop was the *Call-Bulletin*, to confer with my new assistant, Stan Raycraft.

28
Mandark, Man of Mystery

Stan's greatest asset was persistence. While his fellow reporters worked at a frenzied pace to meet a deadline, Stan was slow and steady, and usually late to turn in a story. But once he engaged his mental gears, there was no stopping him.

The *Call-Bulletin* was downtown on the 800 block of Howard Street. Housed in a dull, brown building, it sat next to other dull, brown buildings. I climbed its two granite steps, worn from years of shoe leather coming and going through its two front doors.

I gumshoed my way to the newsroom, where the din of typewriter keys was deafening; the sound of tiny hammers forging words on paper. A sign made to look like a pointing finger guided me to a flight of stairs. "Morgue" it said. I went down the first flight, took a 90 degree turn down another short flight, and I was standing in a basement of concrete columns. Hundreds of bound issues of the *Call-Bulletin* lined the walls on floor to ceiling shelves.

Five mission style tables had piles of loose newspapers, crumpled hamburger wrappers, and bound volumes pulled from the shelves and never put back. Stan popped up from behind a stack of large volumes at one of the tables.

"Hi, ho, big daddy! Any more kiddie actors on ice today?"

"All's quiet in the galloping tintypes," I said. "You'd be the first to know if another one keeled over in his soup bowl." I placed a brown paper bag with a pint of Old Ripper next to Stan.

"It's kinda chilly down here," I said. "I brought something to warm you up."

He opened the bag, pulled out the pint. "A bribe! The first one today, and hopefully not the last." He pulled two water-stained glasses off a shelf, wiped them with his shirtsleeve, and filled them halfway. He passed one to me.

"Here's looking at you, kid!"

The shot went down Stan's gullet like a goldfish at a frat party.

"For crying out loud!" he croaked. "What is this stuff?" He checked the label. "Ninety proof, huh? You always did have good taste in booze, Alex."

"I call it liquid encouragement," I said.

"This is icing on the cake, man. I've already hit pay dirt." Stan poured himself another shot, waved his gums at me and threw it back. He puckered his lips, took in a deep breath, and said, "I believe what I've found will be of great interest to you."

"I'm all ears," I said. "Let's have it."

"I checked into that vaudeville act the Asquiths peddled back in the Stone Age," Stan said, wiping his lips with the back of his hand. "Everyone wondered how Mandark, Supreme Master of Magic could be in two places at the same time. Well, it was easy if you knew the trick. There were two of them."

"Two of what?"

"Two Mandarks, Sherlock; that is, two Asquiths." A grin cracked his kisser.

"Twins, Buster, twins! Onslow and Arvin. Identical. All they had to do was wear matching outfits and voila! Mandark appeared instantly whenever and wherever he, or they, wanted to be. Eyewitnesses saw Mandark all over town at the same time. Of course, the witnesses could have been shills, but that doesn't matter. The act was a hit during the First World War.

"Naturally," Stan continued, "they kept their sneaky twinery on the hush hush, since it was their bread and butter. It must have been a real chore keeping it up, though. They couldn't be seen together, ever, and they went to great lengths to keep it that way, especially before and after performances. One of them would get scarce while the other left the building. When the coast was clear, the one in hiding powdered."

"Explain how you uncovered this deep, dark secret if it was so hush hush? And answer me this. According to Iris Asquith, her husband has no living relatives."

"She's not leveling with you is all I can say. Iris was the eye candy of the act, and a source of bitter rivalry between the twins. It was a torrid love triangle that finally boiled over and made the papers when Iris married Onslow. Arvin flipped out and split up the act. That's when the truth came out about them being twins. The brothers went separate ways, claiming irreconcilable differences. They never spoke to one other after that. End of story."

I said: "So, Onslow became a Red and bought a bookshop in Frisco. What happened to Arvin?"

"The rumor mill has him in Halifax, Nova Scotia, working as a longshoreman in self-imposed exile. That's it for my part of the deal, daddy-o. What have you got for me on the Indian Alley Gang bump offs? I can already feel a Pulitzer coming on."

"Okay, Stanley, let's talk motive. Who stands to gain from the Indian Alley Gang's extermination? I'm inclined to let the Gang off the hook, since none of us ever made a penny, other than our original salaries. Our parents squandered that over 25 years ago. Monarch Studios eventually sold the film rights to Hollywood Pictures in 1939. So, a motive for these kills is still elusive."

"Have you figured out where MacGyver fits in?" Stan queried.

"Naturally there's got to be a tie-in," I said, "since he was Monarch Studios' cameraman for the Indian Alley Gang shorts. He wanted me to know about Tubby Manheim's death. He'd heard I was a private dick and wanted to hire me. Why? Because I know the cast of characters, and, like him I worked for Monarch Studios.

"So, here's a theory, Stan. The death scenes so far have come straight out of our movies. It didn't take long to narrow them down to 1924. Not only that, they're happening in sequence, as originally released. *Flying Fish* came first, then *Tubby's Nightmare*, then *Mother's Little Helper*. Another important fact: 1924 was the Indian Alley Gang's final year at Monarch Studios."

Stan was impressed.

"Man oh man, big guy! How do you remember all this stuff?"

"Easy. I re-read my copy of *The Indian Alley Gang Filmography*. Carla Darla put it together and published a limited edition in 1940. She gave a copy to each member of the gang. She lists every film's release date, crew, and cast. She gives a synopsis, too. If my theory is correct, the next murder will be *Laundry Day* because it came after *Mother's Little Helper*."

Stan stared at the floor. "Who's the starring corpse in that one," he asked.

"Bartholomew 'Sniffles' Hasselhoff. In *Laundry Day*, Sniffles' mom tells him he can't play with the other kids until he does the family laundry. The gang is holding club elections that day, and Sniffles wants to be there. Mom gives him a box of laundry soap and goes shopping.

"As soon as Sniffles' mom leaves, the gang decides to help. They figure they can get the laundry done faster if they pour his mom's entire stash of Sudso laundry soap into the washing machine. The machine goes haywire, jumping up and down, throwing suds everywhere. It fills the house so full of suds it's coming out the chimney on the roof. You get the idea."

Stan said: "Shouldn't you let Sniffles in on this?"

There was no need, as the next day proved.

29
Stonewalled

I sneaked into the office in case the Asquith battleaxe was waiting for me. I used the secret door, a handy way to avoid bill collectors and missionaries. Paloma turned off the radio as soon as she saw me. She waved, and pointed toward the waiting room. I followed the direction of her finger.

Yes, it was Iris Asquith, stewing fitfully in one of our two waiting room chairs. I approached and said, "Step into my lair, said the spider to the fly."

"I'm sure I don't know what you mean by that remark," she griped.

With short, quick steps she clicked into my office, clickity click click, settling gingerly into the client's chair.

"Mrs. Asquith, you've been holding out on me again," I said point blank. "You told me your husband had no living relatives. Fact is, he has a twin brother, Arvin, who was part of your Vaudeville act. Not only that, your husband and Arvin had a falling out because of you."

I torched a Chesterfield, exhaled, and waited. I could hear Asquith's mental machinery gnashing out a response behind those bleary, blue peepers.

"There was no reason to dredge up painful details about our family history," she said. "That was a long time ago. Doing so is a waste of time and money. That has nothing to do with Onslow's disappearance."

"Let me be the judge of what's relevant to your husband's disappearance," I said. "A lead can come from anywhere, now or long ago. For all I know, you've held back one of the best leads in your husband's disappearance."

"I hate to disappoint you, Mr. Blade," the silver-haired quail crooned. "Arvin moved to Nova Scotia decades ago. I've given you a substantial retainer, and your work has been disappointing, to say the least."

"I'm perfectly willing to return your retainer if you're unhappy with our service. I still say you should notify the police. They have the manpower to offer quicker results than my one-man operation."

"No! I told you before, no police. He must be found discretely. Onslow is a very private man. He would be mortified if the police tracked him down."

"He might think otherwise if he's in trouble," I said. "I've checked the Sacramento and San Francisco hospitals, and not one has a record of Onslow Asquith, nor anyone fitting his description, for the last three weeks.

"Your choice of Onslow over Arvin caused a permanent split between them. Revenge is a great motive for skullduggery, even after all these years. Has Arvin contacted either of you since he moved to Nova Scotia?"

"No, he has not. But if you suspect Arvin is a threat, I wish you'd get serious about finding Onslow."

The old crow knew more than she was letting on. If I hadn't already spent her retainer, I'd return it and be done with her.

"What else have you been holding back, Mrs. Asquith?" I prodded.

"I just don't understand it," she blathered aimlessly. "You were so clever in the movies. I don't know what's happened to you. In any case, you must find Onslow. Don't disappoint me, Mr. Blade."

With that, she stood up, clutching her handbag to her bosom. She turned and marched out the door. I listened to the click click of her heels fading down the hall until peace returned to the Mayfair Building.

30
The Next Shoe to Drop

With Iris Asquith out of her hair, Paloma turned the radio back on. After a Sudso laundry soap commercial, the daily news covered the usual post-war drama. The Los Angeles cops were stumped by the so-called 'Moon Slayer' murders. A riot broke out among female strikers at a Los Angeles shoulder pad factory.

"And finally," the newscaster crooned, "we have sad news for fans of Hollywood's beloved Indian Alley Gang." The hair on the back of my neck stood at attention. I bolted from my chair and glued my ears to the Zenith.

"Bartholomew 'Sniffles' Hasselhoff, 33, was found dead yesterday in his Santa Cruz, California home. Hasselhoff was employed as a midway supervisor at the Santa Cruz boardwalk. A private funeral service is planned later this week."

Too late to save Sniffles! I had a few bucks of Asquith's retainer left to invest in a tank of gas. I turned to Paloma, grabbed her by the shoulders.

"This case is getting too close to home!" I yelped. "Hold the fort, Legs; I'm going to Santa Cruz. I'll be back later today if all goes well."

Paloma's gorgeous map looked worried.

"Are you kidding me? Mrs. Asquith is breathing down your neck. You've spent her entire retainer on someone else's case. You've got to come up with a lead, joy boy, and I mean fast." Paloma may dance with a bubble in the buff, but when it comes to business, she's as straightlaced as they come.

"Don't worry," I said. "I'm telling you I'll be back before Iris knows I'm gone. And as soon as I'm back, I'll dig up Onslow. I'll call when I get to Santa Cruz."

At that, I sprinted down the stairs, hopped into my bucket and thumbed the starter. The flathead growled once, twice, then let out a roar. I took Geary to the Cliff House, rounding the curve to the Ocean Beach sea wall. The Great Highway lay before me.

I didn't mention it to Paloma, but I'd also spent Iris Asquith's retainer on new tires for the Terraplane. I replaced its pre-war balding rubber with new Superlux balloon tires. They hummed contentedly on the Great Highway as they drove by sand dunes covered in pink and yellow ice plant. Sand blew across the road, collecting in tiny dunes on the shoulder.

I engaged the Terraplane's Electric Hand, a factory option that allowed me to sit back and drive instead of clutching and shifting manually. At Linda Mar Beach, the engine revved higher as the robot hand downshifted on a hill thick with eucalyptus.

I souped the cylinders on the straightaway near Pigeon Point lighthouse to make time. At the Santa Cruz city limits the highway became Mission Street, heading directly into town. Finally, after more than two hours behind the wheel, I dropped anchor at the *Santa Cruz Sentinel*.

An old drinking buddy of mine worked there, a reporter named Dan Wilson. As luck would have it, our paths crossed in front of the *Sentinel*. He had a mug of coffee in one hand and a notepad in the other. Like Stan Raycraft, he had the look of a well-groomed laundry bag. It was a warm day in Santa Cruz and he'd shed his coat and tie. Dan spotted me first.

"Holy smoke! Is that you Buster Blade? Let me guess. You're here about Sniffles. Am I right, or am I right? More importantly, how about a quote from a former Indian Alley Gang member?"

"Okay, Dan. Here it is: 'Sniffles' passing was a shock to this Indian Alley Gang alumnus. He was a swell guy on and off the set. He'll be sorely missed by those of us who haven't died yet.'"

"Hmm. How about fleshing out that last line, Buster."

"It's nothing, Dan. Sniffles' death has me feeling my age, I guess."

"Okay, I'll massage it a bit if that's okay with you," Dan said, thankfully not pressing further. "You know, they say most deaths occur by accidents in the home. But Sniffles' accident...boy! That was a doozey. I read the coroner's report. He died at home is true, but you'll never guess how."

"Was it laundry day?" I replied.

"How'd you know?"

"I've got sources on the inside, Dan. Please continue. There's got to be more."

"You bet there is! He passed out after putting a boatload of laundry soap in the washing machine. The damn thing overflowed and filled his laundry room from floor to ceiling with foam. He passed out in there and suffocated. Maybe he had one too many. Accidental death, the cops say."

"I don't suppose the police suspect this could have been more than an accident?"

"Not from what they've told me. It's pretty strange, huh? You think there's more to it?"

"Not sure, Dan, but you'll be the first to know when I find out."

Dan had deadlines to meet, so I walked back to the coupe and drove west on Pacific Avenue until I saw the beach.

Sniffles lived at the Sleep Tight Court on Ocean Street, a few blocks from the boardwalk where he worked. I parked in front of The Sleep Tight, torched a gasper and settled behind the wheel. *Laundry Day*.

"Damn," I thought, "what was the name of the picture that came after *Laundry Day*? As soon as I get back to the office, I'll check my filmography."

The boardwalk's summer season was over, but the weather was still warm and kids were screaming their tonsils out on the Giant Dipper. I heard the carousel's band organ playing a snappy Sousa march.

Sniffles' courtyard hovel was a grim reminder of the fate former movie mop tops faced when their stars burned out. Built before the First War, the Sleep Tight was a low rent bungalow court of clapboard cottages. Weeds grew where lawns used to be. Two threadbare palm trees flanked the entrance.

Sniffles' bungalow was at the far end of the court, but unlike Swifty's farmhouse, the door was locked. I was cupping my hands against the front window for a look-see, when I sensed eyes boring into my backside. I turned and saw a wrinkle-faced frail in a cotton housecoat sizing me up from her front porch.

Her facial wrinkles danced an angry jig as she gave me an icy glare. I later determined her look of annoyance was a permanent feature. A blue paisley scarf covered her badly dyed brown hair, which was looped around big, pink hair curlers.

"I'm the manager here," the sourpuss barked. "Can I help you?" Translated that meant I'd better have a real good reason for snooping. I flashed my buzzer, tilting it into the sun for a little extra sparkle.

She gave it a gander, then groused in a tone to match her wrinkles, "I've told the police everything I know!"

She assumed I was the law, and I was, in a private capacity. I slipped the badge into my coat pocket with a flourish.

"I'd like to re-examine the room where the accident took place, Missus ..."

"Miss," she corrected. "Miss Fitch."

"Miss Fitch," I echoed. "I know how tired you must be of officers bothering you with questions, but if you could go over the events of that day just one last time, I'd be grateful."

She seemed miffed, but I could tell she liked attention.

"Well, for you, I'll tell it once more; but this is the last time, and I mean it! I was putting Filbert, my cat, out for the night when I heard a hissing sound coming from Mr. Hasselhoff's cottage. That's when I noticed foam seeping out from under his front door. I knew something was wrong so I called the police. When they got here, I used my passkey to let them in. The house was absolutely *full* of soap bubbles. I've never seen anything like it. They found Mr. Hasselhoff on the back porch, dead. It was horrible. The police pulled him out, but it was too late. And he was so happy before this terrible thing happened."

"Why was that, Miss Fitch?"

"The Bendix people gave him a brand-new washing machine. They wanted him to endorse their latest model in a series of advertisements. He was a well-known child movie star in silent pictures, you know. Sure enough, two men in coveralls delivered a new Bendix the very next day, the day before the accident."

I said, "You've been very helpful, Miss Fitch. Would you mind if I took a quick look around his bungalow?"

The manager edged her way down the front steps as if she were descending Mt. Everest, gripping the handrail and keeping close tabs on her feet. She wobbled across the sidewalk, took a key from her housecoat, and unlocked Sniffles' front door. She gave me the key.

"Lock the door when you leave, and return the key to me. That's all I ask," she said.

"I'll remember, and thank you." She gave me one last scowl and hobbled into her bungalow, shutting the door behind her.

Sniffles' house was still damp and smelled of soap fragrance. The back porch had barely enough room for a washing machine and sink. A clothesline drooped from one end of the porch to the other.

The murder weapon was at the far end of the porch — a brand new 1947 Bendix washer with a spin cycle. This was not the old, pre-war type machine with rollers to hand crank wet clothes through it. A hose on the back of the washer hooked over the sink for drainage. The porch windows faced the boardwalk, but they were all closed.

Somewhere between the wash and spin cycle Sniffles passed out. That's when his lungs filled with soapy death. The coroner found barbiturates in his system, Dan said, which would explain the blackout. The perp behind these murders was an artist, no doubt about it.

The cops just removed enough suds to pull Sniffles out, but my feet still sank up to their bunions in soap bubbles. They sizzled and popped with every step I took. As far as I could tell, the cops had still not connected Sniffles' death with any of the others. It was only a matter of time, though. I knew Stan was dying to get his mitts on that Pulitzer. I also knew the *Banning Record* and the *Santa Cruz Sentinel* would eventually compare notes.

Tossed into a waterlogged corner, a dozen limp boxes of Sudso laundry detergent oozed their soapy innards. It boggled the mind what the cops considered an accidental death these days.

I began to hunt for clues. I checked behind the framed pictures on the walls. I looked inside kitchen cabinets, under carpets, behind and under every dresser drawer, and flushed the toilet and checked inside the tank. Maybe the cops had overlooked something.

I hit pay dirt in the kitchen. Lying on the floor was a damp piece of 35mm film exactly like the one I'd found in Banning. I put it in my pocket. There was more. Sniffles wrote his appointments next to the telephone on the wall.

I looked for recent notations. "SC Appliance, Monday, noon," seemed fresh. Next to that, I noticed a peculiar note. "Film shoot Tuesday, three PM." I copied them on my note pad, locked the front door, and crossed the sidewalk to Miss Fitch's cottage. I knocked, and she cracked the door just enough for me to see that her frown hadn't budged.

"Yes?"

"Returning your key, Miss Fitch; thanks. I just have two final questions. You called in your report last Tuesday, is that correct?"

"I'll never forget it. Yes, it was Tuesday evening."

"Did Mr. Hasselhoff have any visitors earlier that day, say around three o'clock?"

"Yes, I believe so. I was on my way to the store when I passed two men walking up to his front porch."

"Can you describe them?"

"I only saw them for a few seconds when I walked by. One was nicely dressed, very sharp. He wore a gray fedora and a dark blue suit. He had a beard and he walked with a cane. It looked to me like the cane was mostly for show. I can't tell you what the other one looked like, but he wore a cap and carried a movie camera and tripod on his shoulder. Mr. Hasselhoff said the Bendix Company was sending someone to take a short movie of him for an ad campaign."

On a hunch I reached into my pocket and pulled out the photo of Onslow Asquith his wife had given me.

"Is this the man you saw that day?" The spinster took the photo, adjusting her wire frames on her thin nose. "It does resemble him I think. But the man in the picture isn't dressed as nicely as the man I saw."

"Thanks, Miss Fitch, you've been a great help."

I followed the concrete sidewalk back to my heap. The nearest phone booth I could find was in front of the Casa del Sol Apartments across the street from the boardwalk. I dialed Paloma and told her I had one more errand to run before heading home.

The booth had a phone book that wasn't completely torn apart, so I checked the Yellow Pages. Under "Washing Machines," I found Santa Cruz Appliance. The shop was on Mission, the same route I would take back to Frisco.

31
Gladstone Blackstone

Santa Cruz Appliance carried all the major brands: Amana, Maytag, Kenmore, and, of course, Bendix. They had stoves, hot water heaters, refrigerators, fans, and sump pumps, making Santa Cruz Appliance the go-to appliance store.

I flashed my badge at the young man behind the counter and, like Miss Fitch, he pegged me as a cop. Citizens of small towns are a trusting lot.

The young man wore khaki pants and a plaid short-sleeved shirt with the cuffs rolled up. His crew cut hair had that bleached blond look you find in most California beach towns.

"Yes officer," the young man said. "How may I help you?"

"Your shop delivered a Bendix washing machine to a Mr. Bartholomew Hasselhoff on Ocean Street last week," I said. "I'd like to see the invoice for that order if I may."

"Not a problem," he said. "I'll check our recent orders."

He retreated to the office. Through the open door I saw him pull a folder from the top drawer of an oak filing cabinet. He brought it back to the counter.

"Yes, here it is. A Bendix Deluxe, $149.95. It's a fine machine, very well made. The price includes installation and an in-home demonstration on its use. We want our customers to use their machines the way they were intended. They get better results that way. Our tutorials get high marks."

He handed the order to me, and continued his monologue.

"I read about Mr. Hasselhoff's accident," he said. "What I don't understand is why he used so much detergent in one load. They said intoxication may have been involved. We advise customers not to operate their machines while under the influence."

I checked the name on the invoice. Gladstone Blackstone of the Bendix Corporation placed the order.

I looked up at the young man. "Who took this order?"

"I did," he said. "Mr. Blackstone placed the order by phone. A courier delivered a postal money order the same day."

I returned the invoice and thanked the clerk for his cooperation. It looked like a dead end, but I had to be sure. I climbed into the coupe and drove a few blocks down Mission. A Flying A service station had a public phone. I parked the Terraplane next to the booth, went inside and shoved a tribe of Indian head nickels into the slot. I dialed Stan Raycraft's number at the Call-Bulletin and he picked up on the second ring.

"Raycraft talking."

"Stan, it's Alex. I'm in Santa Cruz. I've got a rush job that might help your Pulitzer. Can you find out if a Gladstone Blackstone of the Bendix Corporation was planning an ad campaign with a filmed endorsement from Bartholomew Hasselhoff? It's important."

"You got it, big daddy. When'll you be back in big town?"

"I'll call you in the morning, and thanks." I hung up and nudged the coupe into traffic heading north on the coast highway.

32
Beethoven

The next morning I overslept and got to the office later than usual. First order of business was to find my copy of *The Indian Alley Gang Filmography*. It wasn't with my collection of *Amazing Stories* and it wasn't in my stack of *Dan Turner, Hollywood Detective*. Paloma would know where to look, but she wasn't here. She'd left behind a handwritten note on her desk.

"St. James wants to see you in his office, PRONTO. I mean NOW, Alexander."

Ouch! She calls me Alexander when I'm in hot water, and if St. James wants a pow-wow, the kettle's boiling over. I'd grown fond of my private investigator's license so I decided to motor over to Homicide.

I found St. James at his desk staring at a stack of official looking forms. He wasn't reading them. He was listening to a Beethoven piano sonata on his portable phonograph. He grunted at me.

"Oh, it's you," he grumbled. "I might have known you'd come in at the best part."

"Is this a bad time? I thought you wanted to see me."

He seemed distant, paler than usual. He shushed me.

"Listen!" He stuck a finger in the air and held it there.

After a couple of awkward moments, I said: "Is this a music listening booth or the office of Lt. St. James? Maybe I'm in the wrong room."

He ignored me another minute before he spoke.

"Beethoven! Brilliant, isn't he? Oh, I forgot. You wouldn't know. You're a Rusty Draper fan. In this piece, Beethoven managed to replicate an entire orchestra with one instrument — his piano. You hear that? The trills are the flutes, and the bass line mimics a cello?"

My blank mug ruined his ecstasy. He stood up, lifted the needle off the spinning record. With a wan look, he closed the lid and sighed.

"Oh, the ignorance true genius must endure. Okay, Philo, where were you the morning MacGyver got iced?"

"Oh, I see. I'm under suspicion now, is that it?"

"Why not? You conveniently forgot to mention the mystery deaths of your silver screen playmates when I picked up MacGyver the other day."

I slapped a surprised look on my pan.

"Don't play dumb with me, Buster! You've been getting around. I heard about the trips to Banning and Santa Cruz. And what a coincidence! That's where two of your Hollywood chums came to their untimely ends."

"Unless the papers got it wrong," I replied, "those deaths were accidental. And yes, they were my friends, but there's no law that says I can't ask a few questions about what happened to them. The newspaper accounts were pretty thin on details."

"Cut the malarkey, Blade! You're talking to a city homicide detective, not one of those small-town hicks who got his badge from a cereal box. I'm willing to bet your PI's license that every one of those deaths was murder. That's why you kept it to yourself. You're hiding something. What is it?"

St. James wanted to solve this case fast, and he knew I was part of it.

Before I opened my mouth, he continued. "I did a little digging after reading that obit MacGyver brought. That's when I connected the other deceased members of your film gang. Apparently, Hasselhoff's name was on the list. And within the last six months, their names were crossed off the list. Not only did you know the stiff in your waiting room, you knew every one of the deceased Hollywood has-beens piling up in morgues up and down the state. That puts you on the spot as the potential perp, peeper!"

"I suppose that's one way to look at it," I said, calmly lighting a Chesterfield. "But it's not how I see it. Yeah, I knew them. We were pretty tight when we were kids, but that was 25 years ago. As for covering up their deaths, anyone with a nickel to buy a newspaper could've read about them. Sniffles even made the evening radio news. At the risk of being nosy, Lieutenant, what's my motive?"

"You've done a damn good job keeping that on the QT, I'll grant you that. But if you've got one, I'll find it."

"Do you really believe I committed killery with lethal soap bubbles? Or that I whipped up a batch of taffy and turned Swifty into a human candied apple?"

"I'll admit I'm stymied, and that burns me up. Let me put a bee in your bonnet, Buster. Even if your name's not on my suspects list, you can be damn sure it's on the killer's list of coming attractions. Have you given that any thought, Wonder Boy?"

"That thought has crossed my mind," I confessed. "But I've got no time for thinking like that. I've got a missing person case that's been driving me batty, and I spent the client's retainer on other investigations. Now she's raising Cain."

St. James was anything but sympathetic. He said:

"And I don't blame her! As a small business owner, that kind of behavior can get you bad marks from the Better Business Bureau. But getting back to me, I get real cranky when a homicide goes unsolved for more than 48 hours, and the MacGyver case has exceeded that. It spoils my image. If you find anything new on these deaths, I want to hear about it. Have I made myself clear? Oh, and if you don't come forward, we real cops call that withholding evidence. Ever hear of it?"

"Okay, okay, since you've been so nice to me today, I'll volunteer an observation. But that's all it is, strictly an observation."

St. James clasped his hands behind his head and leaned back in his swivel chair.

"Amaze me."

Since he asked for it, I told him about Sparky's death and how it connected up with our movie *Flying Fish*. I also told him about Swifty and *Mother's Little Helper*. It was a clue, like I said, just not my only clue. It sounded crazy as I heard myself telling it. When I'd finished, St. James made a face like he'd been sucking a lemon.

"That's it? It's a conspiracy about your old kiddie movies?"

"Like I said, it's an observation; something to think about. Mind if I go now?"

"I would like nothing better, but since you're my late best friend's nephew, let me give you a piece of advice. Watch yourself. You've got a big, fat bull's-eye on your back, Buster."

I closed St. James' office door, and lit a cigarette. I lingered and listened. I heard him dialing the phone. He put a tail on me. I guess St. James was hoping I'd lure in the big fish so he could sink his hook. He was the fisherman and I was the bait.

I called Stan Raycraft from a cop pay phone down the hall. He picked up right away.

"Raycraft on this end."

"Stan, it's Alex. What have you got on the Bendix boondoggle?"

"Well, Big Daddy, the Bendix receptionist put me in touch with a Mr. Fantz in their PR department. Not only is there no Gladstone Blackstone working for the Bendix Corporation, but Fantz knew nothing about any ad campaign featuring Sniffles Hasselhoff."

"As I suspected. Thanks, Stan."

"Hold on, Buster, there's more! I crosschecked the name Gladstone Blackstone, and bingo! Turns out he was an old-time Vaudevillian, a magician. I found his name on a 1918 Sutro's double bill along with ... drum roll please? Mandark, Supreme Master of Magic. How does that grab you, Hawkshaw?"

"Your Pulitzer's shaping up, Stan."

33
Love

I'd been so edgy I got into the habit of using the secret door to sneak into the office. I can see who's in the waiting room without them seeing me, and today I piped a big, burly lug. His vacant stare was disconcerting. He seemed to be gazing at something we mortals can't see. His hair was trimmed short on the sides, but shaved down to bare skin on top. It gave him the look of a monastic. His wide tie with extra-large knot stopped mid-way down his barrel chest, and his plaid coat and trousers were louder than an air raid siren. He looked like a stuffed, plaid haggis.

I slipped inside and grabbed the desk phone. I dialed Paloma.

"Who's the gorilla, Legs?"

"He says he represents Reverend Peace It's Wonderful Brown, who wishes to speak with you."

"When it rains it pours. Okay, send him in."

I sat behind my government surplus desk, and the plaid gorilla lumbered in.

"Alexander Blade, I presume?" the lug quipped shoving out a beefy mitt.

"The same. And you are?"

"I am Love."

"*Mr.* Love?"

"Love, no mister, Mr. Blade. As you heard, I am here on behalf of the Reverend Peace It's Wonderful Brown."

"Oh, you mean Luther Brown? When we worked at Monarch Studios he went by the name of Biscuits. I hear he got religion and opened a church."

"Yes, Luther Biscuits Brown was the Reverend's former incarnation, before the Vrilians made him The Earthly Emissary," the beefo jabbered. "It is because of your knowledge of 'Biscuits' that the Reverend wishes to speak with you. He says the past has joined the present, and you know what that means."

"I do?" I pinched myself. The date on my calendar seemed to be correct.

"How does the Reverend know all this, Love?"

"It's the Vrilians," he blathered. "But Reverend wishes to explain in person. He does not trust telephonic devices. His chauffeur will pick you up at three o'clock this afternoon, if that is satisfactory."

I hemmed; I hawed a little too.

"To be honest, Love, I'm working a case, and it's taking a lot of time."

The bald man's features had the look of a mortician handing a corpse the bill for its own funeral.

"In the grand scheme of things, Mr. Blade, there is only *one* case."

Call me a sucker, but the lug intrigued me, and I hadn't seen Biscuits in years, so, I played along.

"And what exactly do the Vermilions want with me?"

"Vrilians, they are called Vrilians, from the planet Vril."

"In any case, what do they want, Love? They always want something."

"All I can tell you is, the Reverend is privy to esoteric information the average Earthman is not privy to. He will explain everything."

"Okay, Love. Have the limo ready for blast off in front of the Mayfair at three," I said.

The bald-headed blister beamed, "Very well, very well indeed, Mr. Blade! I will inform the Reverend you're coming."

At that, he disappeared lickity blip down the hall and was gone. The lingering scent of patchouli oil convinced me I hadn't been dreaming.

34
Biscuits Brown

Back when Biscuits was a star in the galloping snapshots, he and his family lived in a Los Angeles neighborhood so dangerous you could get knifed for owning a wooden nickel. That's why his parents kept him under lock and key. His salary supported the entire family; that included his parents, grandparents, and six brothers and sisters. The only time his dad allowed him out of the house was when the Monarch Studios jitney took him to the studio.

Biscuits' father, Cornelius Brown, a street preacher, spent weekends saving souls in front of Clifton's Cafeteria in downtown LA, and it looked as though Cornelius passed on the religion gene to his son Luther.

At three on the nose, a midnight blue pre-war Packard with dual side mounts came barreling my way. The Packard swung a wide U turn in front of the Mayfair, coming to a stately rest at the curb. I could barely hear the Packard's twelve cylinders purring under a hood as long as the Queen Mary.

A smartly dressed, colored chauffeur with marcelled hair got out, walked around the back of the car and opened the passenger door. He waited for me to step inside. I stepped inside. All street noise vanished when he closed the door. Curtains blacked out the rear windows, all but the one next to me, which was left open. A ceiling light illuminated the plush wool upholstery and thickly padded seats. Cut glass flower vases filled with rose buds hung on the doorposts. Biscuits was doing all right for himself, yes, indeed.

We drove in dead silence along San Pablo Avenue, heading for the North Bay. The road snaked through an oil refinery in Rodeo, skirted a coke plant in Selby, finally rounding a curve that opened up a panoramic view of the Napa River and Mare Island Naval Shipyard. At the Carquinez Bridge, we entered the Vallejo city limits at 3:45. The chauffeur's timing was impeccable.

The Barrel Club, shaped like a huge, two-story whiskey barrel, faced the Lincoln Highway. From there we turned on to Georgia Street and drove west toward the waterfront.

Biscuits' Northern California headquarters was on the 300 block of Georgia Street, across from the New York Loan Company, a bright red pawnshop with its name in big, white letters across the front. Biscuits' ran a string of churches with missions, in San Pedro, Pismo Beach, San Jose, and here in Vallejo. The Hollywood tabloids dutifully kept tabs on Biscuits' spiritual journey from the very beginning. He made good copy, and reporters loved him.

According to the papers, Biscuits became an outer space emissary in 1940, when a mind-altering experience changed his life forever. Late one evening while fishing near Pismo Beach pier, a massive, black zeppelin suddenly appeared, hovering directly above him. Paralyzed with fright, Biscuits came to his senses when an explosion from the zeppelin filled the air with floating debris.

He saw hundreds of diaphanous disks drifting down to the beach. Within minutes, the disks began to fade, and ultimately vanish. He picked up one of the disks before it disappeared and had just enough time to study it.

When *Hollywood Confidential* interviewed him, Luther described the disk as having a portrait of Felix the Cat on one side, and a Tibetan swastika on the other. The disk put him in telepathic contact with the zeppelin's commander, he said, who told Luther his ship had come from the planet Vril.

It was only the first chapter of Luther's spiritual journey. As the last disk dissolved on the sand, a bolt of energy shot through his gray matter, imparting some sort of universal knowledge. He blacked out. Forty-eight hours later, he woke up in San Luis Obispo General Hospital, where he began to write his book of prophecy. He called it *Peace, It's Wonderful,* and used the title as his new moniker. Luther Biscuits Brown was no more. He had a new identity now — Peace, It's Wonderful.

The Vrils contacted him again, while he was visiting his sister in Carpentaria. This time they invited him to come aboard. They took him to their home planet Vril, where Luther met the Vrilian Elder Council.

The Elders gave him the lowdown. The military's reports of so-called flying saucers were, in truth, Vrilian observation ships. Our atom bomb blasts came to the Vrilians attention in 1945, when we detonated the first ones. Humans now posed a serious threat to the solar system, and ultimately the universe. So, the Vrils came up with a plan to temper our violent ways with a peace virus.

To initiate the plan, they appointed Luther as their emissary. A ceremony followed, wherein Luther ate a paté of Vrilian grubs infected with the virus. Luther became disoriented and suddenly found himself back in Carpentaria. Within a week he founded the Interplanetary Church for All Creatures. His followers, also called Vrilians, number about 2200 mostly rich, mostly white little old ladies from Southern California.

I hadn't seen or heard from Luther since 1932, long before his transformation. That was the year we made our infamous comeback film. "Uncle" Bud Crossman decided an Indian Alley Gang reunion picture would appeal to former fans who'd reached their teen years like we had. *Hollywood High Jinx* was the Gang's first and only talkie. They should have called it *Hollywood High Stinks*. It was the biggest box office bomb of 1932. Within a week of the release we were out of work, which was hardly a novelty by that time.

Peace It's Wonderful's chauffeur pulled up to the Vallejo branch of the Interplanetary Church for all Creatures, got out, went around the back, and opened the car door. He escorted me up a narrow flight of stairs, leaving me in an anteroom with chairs that lined the walls from corner to corner. A high-yellow Vrilian female wearing a colorful sari sat tastefully arranged on the corner of her desk. She conversed with another Vrilian female, also wearing a sari, at the other corner of the desk. They could have been twins. The Vrilian closest to me crossed her legs as I approached. A garter belt and black nylons showed through a split in her sari.

"May I help you, sir?" Her voice was slow like maple syrup.

"Alexander Blade to see Reverend Brown."

"Do you have an appointment?"

"Just tell the Reverend Buster's here. He sent for me."

She slid off the desk, exposing even more thigh.

"Follow me, Mr. Buster?"

I couldn't help but do as she asked. I walked behind her, in her wake of cosmic undulations. We entered a dim chamber, the walls and ceiling draped in purple velvet. A miniature flying saucer glowed on a pedestal in the center of the room. The spacecraft alternated colors between blue, green, and red.

"Make yourself comfortable, Mr. Buster. The Reverend will be with you shortly." The high-yellow space frail disappeared through a hidden opening in the purple drapes.

I sat facing a desk as long as the Graf Zeppelin. In an instant, Luther appeared behind the desk, resplendent in a purple double-breasted suit.

Golden threads glistened throughout the fabric. His hair still had that wild, flyaway look his fans loved.

"Buster! It's so good to see you. How's tricks?"

"If that Packard limo of yours is paid for, I'd say my tricks don't hold up to yours, Luther. I'm still trying to wrap my head around this new racket of yours."

"Just call me 'Peace' for short, Buster, and it's no racket. It's the real deal. I know you remember old down-and-out Biscuits Brown, right? After Monarch Studios gave us the boot, I was washed up, a boozer, a loser. I was fishing for my dinner the day the white light came. Now, here I am, a descendant of the prophets who came before me. I ask you Buster; how could Biscuits pull this off without some serious cosmic intervention?"

"Don't ask me, Peace, I haven't read your book. I'm still trying to wrap my head around OAHSPE. My secretary says it holds the key to all knowledge."

"OAHSPE was fine in its day, Buster, but now we've got an open hotline to the Vrilians. With the space brothers' help, we'll usher in a new age here on Earth. But forget all that. I want to explain why I asked you here. The hotline's gotten so hot lately it's caught fire. Word from the space brothers has it that something big and bad is going down, and it involves you, me, and the rest of the gang."

"You might say we're on the same page, Peace," I confirmed. "I was in Banning for Swifty's sendoff last week. I suppose you heard about it, and about Sparky's fishing accident, and Sniffles and Tubby. They were accidental deaths, according to the cops, but as far as I'm concerned it was pre-meditated murder."

I knew why Luther was concerned, and I couldn't blame him. Maybe he traveled to planet Vril and maybe he didn't. But here on planet Earth, life was sweet for Peace It's Wonderful Brown. I reached for a Chesterfield and offered one to the Rev.

"No thanks, Buster. I gave 'em up. It's a toxic plant; poisons the mind."

"Mind if I poison mine?"

"It taints your celestial pulchritude, but why not? I wouldn't interfere with your chosen path to enlightenment."

"Let's nix the high-toned homilies, Peace. Remember me? It's your old buddy Buster. Give it to me in plain Earth lingo, okay? What's the message the space bros want to impart?"

"The problem is," he began, "it takes a little fancy footwork to decipher their messages. But I have the inside track on that, having met them."

"Inquiring minds would like to know how you get these messages in the first place," I said.

"I know it sounds crazy to a non-believer, Buster, but sometimes they communicate through the radio. They broadcast on a sub frequency during the Major Bow's Amateur Hour. Other times it's during The Jack Benny Show. I've been told that Rochester is a Vrilian double agent.

"But with the advent of television and its commercials, they've begun to communicate through those. Other times I just sit at the typewriter and type what they dictate, kind of like automatic writing. Their latest message, a warning, came to me in a dream. That's their third method of communication."

"I hope it's better than mine. What's the dream?"

"I saw a castle with seven towers. A king lived in the castle, but the king was our former director, Thorner von Einsburg. He spoke to me. He said 'Beware of Cain.' He said Cain wants to harm the gang, and of course, that would include me, the Vrilian emissary, which is why I was forewarned. That's it, Buster. Vrilian messages are usually about the stupidity of the human race, so I'd say this one was real important."

"Okay, I'll take a stab at it," I said. "We both know von Einsburg lives on the laughing farm up north. That could be the castle in your dream. What's *your* interpretation?"

"Well, Cain was Abel's brother, and Cain killed Abel. But the Cain and Abel parable is similar to early Sumerian legends of Enkimdu and Dumuzi, who competed for the love of Inanna, a fertility goddess. In other words, von Einsburg could know of others involved in this plot. In any case, I think you should go to the castle. Talk to von Einsburg. He will clarify my dream, I'm sure of it."

"That's a pretty thin lead, Peace. But, you're right. I need to talk to von Einsburg. He may be crazy but it's worth a shot."

"If you like, my chauffeur will drive you there tomorrow."

"That's okay, I'll take my heap. Just have him drop me back at the office. Meanwhile, keep a bodyguard with you at all times, okay, Peace?"

"A bodyguard is part of my daily attire, Buster. In parting, let me say that I hope one day you'll be filled with the almighty spirit of Vril's green planet."

"Me too. Green has always been my favorite color," I said.

We gave the Indian Alley Gang handshake for old time's sake, and Biscuits Brown vanished behind the purple curtains.

35
Where Birds Die

The Terraplane was feeling poorly today. It took three tries before it coughed up a hairball and fired on all six cylinders. It's still adjusting to post-war gas. We were on our way to the Napa State Hospital insane asylum to see my former director, Thorner von Einsburg.

I followed the same route I'd taken yesterday, but when I reached Vallejo, I took Highway 29, the road to take me to the nut farm von Einsburg called home.

The last time I saw him we were on the set of *Baby Bwana*, a quarter of a century ago. I wondered if he'd even remember my name. He sure as hell wouldn't recognize me. I'd changed since then.

An ancient rock wall paralleled the road as I neared the small town of Napa. A clock tower loomed above the trees in the distance. I turned off the highway and passed under a rock arch that put me on the long, straight promenade to the massive sanitarium.

Lush, well-tended gardens softened the brooding vibrations that oozed from the castle like steam from a pressure cooker. The seven towers from Luther's dream dominated the castle's five-story structure. It practically put Versailles to shame. Vermont slate, Colfax marble, and millions of bricks made up the castle's massive walls.

Here and there patients were raking, trimming, watering the gardens. I couldn't tell if they were happy, sad, or indifferent. They all wore white cotton clothing: baggy pants and shirts for men, simple dresses for women.

I parked the coupe next to a Model A Ford ambulance under a large flowering magnolia. Statues of animals and hooded figures frowned above the main entrance. The four virtues of the ancient Greeks were represented: Fortitude, Justice, Prudence, and Temperance. Chiseled into a stone slab above the door was the motto: "In temperance learn thou to live." But temperance was not what got these people in here. I stepped inside.

The first door on my right was the visitors' check-in. I went in. A brick wall disguised as a man sat at a desk behind a walnut counter. He

pecked at the keys of a typewriter with two fingers, but stood up when he saw me.

He wore the same loose-fitting white clothing as the patients in the garden. His all-white hair was cut so short his sunburned, pink scalp glowed. His eyebrows had mysteriously disappeared. An upper front tooth stood out bright white in a mouth of yellow teeth. It was all I could do to keep from staring at that damn white tooth.

The man seemed happy to see me, almost too happy, like a pack of Jehovah's Witnesses before the door slams shut on them.

With near religious fervor the man said: "Good morning! How may I help you on this beautiful day?"

I smiled. "I've come to visit one of your residents, an old friend of mine. We used to work together. His name is Thorner von Einsburg, formerly of Los Angeles."

The man pulled his invisible eyebrows together as he flipped pages in a leather-bound register.

"Yes, von Einsburg. Room 442, fourth floor, wing C. An attendant will take you to his room. Just sign the visitors' log, please."

He lifted a heavy book from under the counter, spun it round to face me, handed me a pen, and I signed. He flashed his white tooth and said: "I hope you enjoy your visit, Mr. Blade. An aide will come for you shortly."

I stepped outside to loiter under the grimacing gargoyles. I lit a gasper and leaned against the wall, watching white clad patients wander by. Two women strolled arm in arm, singing *Row, Row, Row Your Boat*. A man pushing a wheelbarrow filled with tulip bulbs trudged along behind them, followed by a thin, pale man wearing a leather football helmet. He was looking for butts on the ground. Whenever he found one, he'd study it carefully. If it passed muster, he put it in his coat pocket. Without saying a word, he ran off to catch up with the others.

A short, brown man slipped up behind me so quietly I nearly jumped when I saw him. He introduced himself as Baldemar Dalliwal. His hair was dark, like the circles around his eyes. Poorly drawn tattoos of Hindu gods covered his forearms. He had a strong accent, but was easy enough to understand.

"Hello, my friend," he said cheerily. "Are you staying with us or just visiting?"

"Just visiting," I threw my butt on the ground, crushing it under my shoe.

"My friends call me Baldi," he said. Without changing his light-hearted expression, he began to tell me a story. It was an observation, really, but I sensed it was important to him.

"I am willing to bet, my friend, that you have not seen a single dead bird in your travels today. I am correct?"

I thought about it, and replied, "Now that you mention it, I can't say that I have."

"Of course, you haven't. That is because the birds, they are living in two different worlds. One is the world very high above us, up there." He pointed skyward. "The other is the one very far below, where we are standing now. Understand?"

A dark cloud descended on his countenance. I sensed we were about to run a marathon through the briar patch of his mind.

"Birds do not die in our world. Understand? They fly, they eat, they lay their eggs here and raise their young, but they do not die in this world."

I said: "That's why we aren't walking through piles of dead birds?"

"You catch on fast, my friend! It took me many years to learn this. I had no one to help me think it out. Birds have to die sometime, do they not? We see hundreds, even thousands of them in our daily lives, in the trees, on telephone wires, in the skies. But where are these thousands of dead birds? They are not lying on the ground. Does someone hide them? I think not."

He saw a slight flicker of doubt flit across my pan, so he explained further.

"This is counter intuitive I know, because you have seen dead birds caught by the cat, or birds that flew into a window and broke their necks. These deaths were accidental. But where are the rest? There should be many, don't you agree? No, you don't say, but I will tell you, my friend, and for free, too. They die in a place called Atmospherea. It is in another dimension, one hundred and one miles above Duluth, Minnesota. That is why you don't see them here, dead."

A light snapped on in my cerebral cellar as my thought waves collided with his. He was an OASPHE fan! I came this close to admitting he was onto something when a curly haired young man wearing a white tunic with very large buttons approached me.

"Mr. Blade? I'm Jeff. If you're ready, I'll take you to Mr. von Einsburg's room."

I bid Baldi and his dead birds adieu and followed Jeff under the haunted arch. We trekked for what seemed like miles over highly polished wood floors smelling of Lysol and wax. I saw patients with buckets of soapy water, scrubbing floors with bristle brushes. Other patients followed them on their hands and knees, polishing the wood planks with floor wax and rags. The intense look of concentration on their faces was eerie.

Jeff noticed me watching them and explained. "Most of our patients participate in the work therapy program," he said. "We have our own dairy with milking cows, our own vegetable gardens, and our own chickens. We've been a self-sustaining farm and mental institution since the hospital opened in 1875."

I sensed a touch of pride in Jeff's voice. But 1875 was a long time ago. The building was showing its age. Jeff's castle, tended by its happy residents, was a firetrap with no elevators and no fire escapes. It was an Atom Age antique. Finally, we reached Room 442.

"Here's Mr. von Einsburg's room. I'll let him know you're here." Jeff went inside. In less than a minute he returned. "Go right in. If you need me, there's a phone on the wall over there. Dial 9 and ask for Jeff. They'll page me."

I entered Room 442 where, for the first time in 23 years, I faced Thorner von Einsburg.

36
A Break in the Case

Cracks laced the lathe and plaster walls of his shabby room. A barred window let in just enough light for a melancholy spider to spin its cockeyed web. So, this is where the scion of Monarch Studios had languished since 1924.

A faded Maxfield Parrish print hung crooked above a neatly made hospital bed. A crazy quilt covered the bed. Everything seemed off kilter in here, including its occupant.

I barely recognized von Einsburg, who sat at a small writing table near a window. Mental illness had carved deep canyons into his face, and he'd grown a beard. He wore the white clothing of his fellow inmates.

He studied me with a tinge of paranoia as I approached.

"Who are you and what do you want?" His voice was distant, disembodied. I tried to place it in my memory, but it was too long ago.

"You probably don't recognize me, Mr. von Einsburg. It's been many years. I'm Alexander Blade; you know, Buster Blade, from the Indian Alley Gang?"

His pan was as vapid as a rice cracker.

"You don't look familiar," he said.

I was beginning to think Luther's Vrilians had given me a bum steer. But, in the blink of an eye, the former movie mogul took on a more hopeful tone.

"Have you come to get me out of here?" he asked. "They think I'm loony like all the other kooks in here, but I'm not! Do I look crazy to you?"

Now, I may not know much about psychology, but he looked nutty as a fruitcake. Nevertheless, I played along.

"Don't they treat you well here?" I asked.

"It has nothing to do with that!" he barked. "I am not Thorner von Einsburg. I never was. My brother tricked me, switched places with me. Don't believe any of his Herr von Einsburg crap. His name is Arvin, Arvin Asquith. He made up that 'kraut name so he could make it big in

Hollywood. We're identical twins, but I can't convince the doctors I'm Onslow; Onslow Asquith!"

Come to think of it, his accent was not the same as von Einsburg's, and he vaguely resembled the photo of Iris Asquith's husband. Things were taking an unexpected turn, but I kept my cool.

"In that case, your wife will be happy to know I've found you," I said. "Iris hired me to bring you home. She said you went to Sacramento for a convention and never came back."

"I was shanghaied long before that convention took place," he explained. "Several months ago, Arvin sent me a letter. He said it was extremely important that he speak to me. I couldn't imagine what we had to talk about, since we hadn't spoken in years. I had no idea he was in a mental ward!

"Anyway, when I got here, the first thing I noticed was he'd grown a beard, just like mine. We looked identical again. Arvin had two glasses of lemonade sitting on this table. He proposed a toast to our reunion. I should have known better. Mine was spiked, probably with his medications. When I woke up, he had switched clothes with me and was gone."

"Then you didn't withdraw $1000 from your bank recently?"

"How could I? I've been locked up in here. It had to be Arvin."

"Then I also take it you didn't leave your suitcase at the Hotel Ebner."

"1946 was the last year I stayed at the Ebner. Anyway, let me finish!

When the drugs wore off, I told the doctors it was all a mistake, that I was really Onslow Asquith, not Thorner von Einsburg. They said that's what I'd been telling them for months. They said I was just confused.

"Arvin's always been a vindictive person. He'd obviously

planned the switch for a long time. And now he's free to claim Iris. He always wanted her; hated me for marrying her."

I said: "So Iris thinks Arvin is you? And when he left her a couple weeks ago and didn't come back, she hired me to find him, thinking it was you."

"Of course she thinks it's me," he said. "But I've been here for six or seven months, not a few weeks. It's hard to keep track of time now that I'm forced to take Arvin's anti-psychotic medications. I have trouble remembering. What did you say your name was?"

"Alexander Blade. Buster is the name you, I mean, von Einsburg would have known."

This was getting complicated. A meeting with my former director to discuss Biscuit Brown's dream had turned into the Asquith case. If this guy was really Onslow, it meant my former director was never really Thorner von Einsburg. He was the alter ego of a man named Arvin Asquith.

With desperation in his voice, Asquith pleaded: "If you get me out of this snake pit, I can pay. I have money."

I told him I'd do my best to bring his wayward twin to justice but made no promises. I bid farewell and left room 442 to find Jeff the orderly. He was down the hall with a patient who was flapping her arms like a bird. I queried Jeff about von Einsburg's identity crisis.

"Yes, it was very sad," Jeff replied. "I think it was last December when Mr. von Einsburg told Dr. Inch he was someone named Onslow Asquith. He stopped shaving and grew a beard. It was a new and unexpected chapter in his disorder.

"Dr. Inch believes von Einsburg's personality may have split during one of his shock treatments. We don't know exactly how it happened, but it was an unfortunate setback."

Jeff led me through the maze of hallways back to the Terraplane. I torched a Chesterfield, contemplating the stone bears above their portal to insanity. Was the missing Arvin Asquith really von Einsburg, my former director? Or was von Einsburg masquerading as Onslow Asquith? If the man I saw was really von Einsburg, how would he know about Arvin, Onslow, and Iris Asquith? I thumbed the starter, spun my bucket around, and watched castle Frankenstein disappear in the rearview mirror. I had to analyze these new developments.

37
Distracted

After two shots of Old Ripper, I was still analyzing. As crazy as von Einsburg sounded, his story connected a few dots. Iris Asquith may well have been the victim of a clever shell game. Then again, if she knew that Arvin, aka, von Einsburg, was in the asylum all along, she might be in cahoots with him.

Rather than wait for her to make an appearance, I gave the old bat a jingle. She picked up the phone and her tonsils quavered over the wire.

"This is Mrs. Asquith speaking."

"Blade here. You'll be happy to know I may have located your missing husband, and he's alive and kicking."

Dead silence on her end. Her gray matter must have gone into a tailspin.

"I'm so relieved," she said at last, though not too convincingly. "But what do you mean, you may have found him? Either you found him or you didn't."

"Your husband, if it really is your husband, is registered at the insane asylum in Napa. He said he never came home from the convention because he never got there in the first place. He claims his brother Arvin switched places with him by stealth. That means the man you *think* is your husband may well be Arvin. I suggest you go to Napa State Hospital right away and confirm this man's identity."

"But Arvin is in Nova Scotia," she protested.

"Maybe," I said. "That's the other part of this puzzle. The man I went to see in the asylum was supposed to be my former director, Thorner von Einsburg. He informed me that his twin swapped straitjackets with him, and that Arvin was von Einsburg all along, which came as a big surprise to me. All these years I thought my director was Thorner von Einsburg, not your husband's brother."

"This is too ridiculous for words," the Asquith quail sputtered. "First you couldn't find Onslow, and now you say he's in an insane asylum under an assumed name. You were better as a cowboy, Mr. Blade, not a detective!"

At that, the biddy hung up on me.

I dialed the Homicide Squad, figuring St. James would want to know about this latest wrinkle in the case. He wasn't at the office fawning over his favorite composer, so I left a message with the front desk.

As I was sorting my conundrums, Paloma popped out of her costume parlor in the next room. She was an eyeful that knocked von Einsburg right out of my head. She was preparing for tonight's performance, but was only halfway there. She'd slipped on her nude thong, but had not pasted on her new tassels. Her impressive breastworks swung hypnotically my way.

She arranged herself on my lap, then snaked her arm around my neck. This gave me a birds' eye view of the two biggest stars of Andy Wong's all-Chinese review. The warmth of her firm Latin caboose hardened my arteries.

She cooed: "Can you pick me up after the show tonight, Wonder Boy? I crave company tonight."

"Put your pasties on, Legs! My glands are getting ideas."

"That's the point? How about it?"

"You do realize this blurs the line between employer and employee," I grated. "You'll get me in trouble with the secretarial union."

"Look, I won't tell the union if you won't."

My hormones did a slow crawl up my trouser leg as Paloma polished my tie with her pineapples.

"Okay, okay," I squawked. "I never could say no to a union member. Look for me in the bar after the show. I'll be the guy with a red carnation behind his ear."

38
Farewell, Onslow Asquith

San Francisco had changed after the war. It looked the same as before, but its citizens lived in the shadow of the Great Fear. A Red Menace had replaced the Yellow Peril, and its tentacles were everywhere. Politicians called it the Cold War. They said trust no one. Even movies at the local popcorn palace were suspected of high treason. McCarthy said Stalin's Hollywood minions were slipping the Socialist agenda into Dagwood and Blondie's kitchen chatter. Commie witch-hunts were a national sport, as screenwriters got dragged before holier-than-thou committees accusing them of anti-American activity.

It was a hell of a time to start a detective agency, but it sure beat the crap out of air conditioning. Nobody wanted air conditioning in San Francisco. On the other hand, plenty of folks needed a private dick, especially if the price was right.

Morning brightened the dark corners of my Telegraph Hill apartment, but Paloma and I slept in. She was lying next to me, beginning to stir. She turned over and pressed soft curves into my back.

"Mmmmm, what time is it, Alex?" she purred.

I snored like a harbor seal, and she pinched my arm.

"Huh? What?" I croaked.

"What *time* is it?" I rolled over to face her.

"You mean you're not wearing your watch?" I quipped. Her chassis snuggled closer. I wrapped my free arm around her back. That's when the telephone began to gargle its annoying jingle. My hand slid down Paloma's back, but the phone kept ringing. I finally gave up and answered it.

"Blade talking. I'm kind of busy right now."

"You're never too busy for Leroy St. James, peeper!"

"Oh, it's you, Lieutenant. What's the good word?"

"I just got your message about that loose screw at the state asylum."

"That's right. If he's really who he says he is, it means his twin brother Arvin, that is, my former director, Thorner von Einsburg, pulled a fast one. It also means he's on the loose, and could be shaping up as a person of interest in our case."

"What do you mean *our* case? And where's this nut job now? Have you got any leads?"

"I'm not even sure the guy gave me the straight dope. Don't forget, he's a rooster on the scrambled egg farm. I suggest you flag your derby up there and run him through the ringer. He's not going anywhere."

"I'll do that, Philo, but this better not be a wild goose chase."

As I yakked with St. James, Paloma's nimble fingers were playing hacky sack with little Buster, who begged me to hang up the phone.

"Just listen to the guy's story, Lieutenant. He's a talker, and he wants to get sprung from his cell. You decide if he's nuts or not."

St. James hung up abruptly.

"How about breakfast, sweet stuff?" Paloma purred. "I'll have oysters on the half shell."

Her velvety body clung like static. She was hard to resist, and I didn't want to. Let St. James do the heavy lifting for a change.

After a coed shower where Paloma gratuitously kept dropping the bar of soap, we whipped up brunch — black coffee, eggs over easy, and toast. The butchers' union was on strike, so no bacon. We were lucky to have toast. The bakers' union had settled its strike a few days ago.

We gave the Mayfair a pass and spent the day in North Beach sipping cappuccinos al fresco. We ate spumoni ice cream on a bench in Washington Park and watched the tourists. It was going on four o'clock when we flagged our barking dogs up the Stockton Street tunnel stairs to the Mayfair Building.

We'd no sooner opened the door when the phone clanged like a fire alarm. Paloma sprinted to her desk and picked up.

"Yes, Lieutenant, he's here." Silently, her lips said: "St. James," pointing to the receiver. I went into my inner sanctum and picked up the phone.

"How was the asylum?" I asked.

"Chock full 'o nuts, Sherlock! Where've you been? You know that wing nut you sent me up there to grill?"

"I don't like the sound of this," I said.

"You shouldn't. He's as dead as Hitler's conscience. He'd been that way no more than an hour before I arrived on the scene, a shiv stuck in his wishbone. Naturally, no one heard or saw a thing, and no wonder. The place was crawling with dipsos, nymphos, and psychos."

"Maybe that's why it's called an insane asylum," I quipped.

"Well, he got out, and it's out of my jurisdiction, so the Napa County sheriff has the case. I'll talk to you later, Blade. I got other fish to fry." He rang off.

I stared at the cigarette burns on my desk blotter and listened to traffic on the street below. I dialed Iris Asquith's number. No answer.

39
Niles, California

I was about to pour myself a second round of detective's friend when the phone jangled. Paloma took the call and yelped from her desk:

"Iris Asquith on the line, Alex!"

"Bout time," I groused.

It was Iris Asquith all right, sounding like she'd drunk too much coffee.

"Mr. Blade? Onslow just called. He said he's being followed. He fears for his life. H-he said he's in a town called Niles, in Contra Costa County. Have you heard of it? He needs our help. He's in danger!"

I thought, if the dead man at the asylum was really Onslow, then Arvin is the surviving twin. That means the phone call was from Arvin pretending to be Onslow. Then again, if the dead man in the asylum was Arvin, that meant Onslow needed help. And why Niles? There was only one way to find out.

"Yes, I know where Niles is. Did he tell you where to find him?"

"He said he'd be waiting for us in an abandoned movie studio at Niles and G streets," Asquith quavered.

"That can only be the old Essanay Studios lot," I said. "It was the only film studio Niles had. By the way, did you see the man at the state hospital I told you about?"

"I don't drive, Mr. Blade. So, no, I have not seen him yet."

"Don't bother. Somebody got to him before the police did. He's been murdered."

"Then we're wasting time! We've got to reach Onslow before it's too late!"

"Sorry, there's no we about it, Mrs. Asquith. If your husband's in danger, there's a chance you are too."

"I don't care. I'm paying you and I'm going," she insisted. "I'll meet you at your office in half an hour." She hung up.

Paloma gave me that worried look again.

"Don't forget the yarrow sticks Alex. I have a bad feeling about this. And remember what Reverend Brown told you."

"I'll admit the yarrow sticks and the Vrilians are on the same page," I said. "But don't worry, Kitten. I've got a life insurance policy with six little indemnity clauses." I slipped my .38 police special into its shoulder holster.

"This case is about to break wide open," I said. Once I find out who's waiting for me in Niles, I'll sic St. James on him. Then I can close the door on Iris Asquith!"

Paloma tried harder.

"I don't trust Mrs. Asquith, Alex. She's never been up front with us. She's big trouble."

"This'll be the quickest way to find out," I said. "Don't worry, when we get to Niles, I'll keep my eyeballs peeled for killer taffy machines and such."

"Even that kook Mr. Ching told you to lay off this case," Paloma persisted.

"Have a little faith, Legs. I'll be back in two shakes of a yarrow stick and we'll give Iris Asquith the bum's rush. After that, we'll take a vacation to the Mendocino redwoods."

True to her word, Iris Asquith's taxi arrived at the Mayfair Building right on time. I met her out front, and we piled into my bucket.

Niles was a bit of a drive to the far side of the Oakland hills. A railroad town, it was situated on the old Transcontinental line.

Back in the early days, Niles was a Hollywood outpost in California's hinterlands. The Essanay Film Company cranked out the first cowboy action films, and made audiences holler for more. Charlie Chaplin came along and filmed The Tramp in Niles.

But it didn't last. Essanay went under not long after it lost Chaplin's contract. The movie industry settled in southern California, and Niles shrank to a mere footnote in film history. The Essanay studios were abandoned.

Heading east, I juiced the Terraplane's twin carbs with all the ethyl they could swallow. In Fremont, we veered off Mission Boulevard, drove under a train trestle and headed down Niles Boulevard. We passed the railroad station and the Edison Nickelodeon, a nondescript silent movie theater that used to feature Chaplin films. It was dark inside, and looked like it had been that way a long time.

Finally, the remains of the Essanay movie lot came into view. The main building burned down years ago. A block of modest bungalows for Essanay's married employees survived, along with a few sheds, and a glassed-in shooting stage that took advantage of Niles' perpetual sunlight. The bungalows were privately owned homes now, so it was doubtful Asquith was in one of those.

We skidded to a stop next to a dilapidated fence. If I remembered my movie history correctly, Chaplin filmed *The Champion* on this very spot. I turned to the Asquith wren.

"Okay, Mrs. Asquith, where do we find Onslow?"

"He said he'd be inside a shooting stage. I assume that's it over there, behind the fence." She pointed to the glass structure in the deepening twilight.

"You wait here," I said. "I'll bring him out. Then we'll drive back to Frisco and all will be well. Got it?"

"Yes, of course. Let's get this over with. I'm very nervous out here."

She was fidgeting, as always, with her beaded purse.

40
Spooks and Kooks

Iron Horse Lane was an unpaved alley that separated the Essanay bungalows from the rest of the movie lot. I made my way down the alley past dimly lit back porches. Muffled sounds of radio programs, dishes being washed, and family conversations filled the night air. I found a door in the big, glass structure and slipped in.

Birds had used broken windowpanes to enter the building and fluttered and murmured in the darkness above me. Rotting electrical cables, empty film cans, and broken light stands — relics of Essanay's glory days — littered the building.

Primitive, wooden light stands had fallen victim to vandals. Every light bulb and mirror reflector had been smashed. The broken glass crunched under my brogans, so I stepped with caution. Gaping holes in the floorboards were everywhere. I found no trace of Asquith, so I began to explore other areas. A sliver of light through a crack in the wall caught my attention and I called out.

"Hello! Mr. Asquith! It's Alexander Blade. Iris is in the car. We're ready to take you home!"

I remembered Paloma's yarrow sticks, and slipped my .38 from its holster. I saw a door, with light around the edges. I reached for the knob, pulled it gently toward me with my left hand, the .38 in my right.

As my eyes began to focus, I saw a sight that was crazier than Luther Brown's space ship: a movie set, and a dead ringer for Monarch Studios' Indian Alley Gang short, *Spooks and Kooks*. I recognized it right away as the spooky castle scene. What the hell was it doing here?

Right then, Paloma's warning echoed in my gray matter. Too late. My cranium was bludgeoned from behind, and I saw the kind of stars you don't see on a studio payroll. They were bright, they twinkled, and they followed me down a hole that was darker than the basement of a Chinese delicatessen.

I found myself on the Monarch Studios lot, dressed in a loincloth for my role in *Baby Bwana*. Sitting behind Mr. Jumbles' massive head, I looked down on my director, Thorner von Einsburg. He was arguing with Joe Martin, the studio's animal trainer. They looked different dressed in white robes and hoods, like Uncle Carl.

Von Einsburg wanted Joe Martin to release a flock of flamingos as I rode Mr. Jumbles into the native village. It must have been a last-minute script change.

My director raised his megaphone.

"Speed, Camera, Action!"

Mr. Jumbles lurched in the direction of the native village. Each time the behemoth's feet hit the ground, the impact shot through me like a jolt of electricity. Just ahead, natives streamed out of their huts, spears in hand. They wore white robes and hoods instead of beads and grass skirts. It must have been another one of von Einsburg's last minute script changes.

The natives tossed their spears into a pile and made a bonfire. They held hands and danced around the fire as they sang *The Bright Fiery Cross*. They danced and danced until they were a blur of white light. The spinning light rose into the sky above the fire. I watched it split into several smaller lights. They looked like the newspaper photos of flying saucers.

Biscuits suddenly appeared in front of me, wearing his purple suit. He was five years old again, and the suit was far too large. His sleeves and pant legs piled up in folds on the ground. The suit had tiny white lights blinking on and off in the material.

He told me to wake up; that von Einsburg wanted to wrap up the scene. If I did a good job, he'd tell the space brothers to take me to the planet Vril, where I'd become a saint in the Vrilian Pantheon of Reformed Earthmen.

Before I could ask Biscuits where to find von Einsburg, he disappeared. Paloma stood in his place, holding her bubble. She tossed it into the air, where it floated above her nude body. She spoke to me.

"The yarrow stalks, Alex. Listen to the yarrow stalks or you're a dead man!"

41
The Haunted Castle

I crawled out of the darkness on all fours, nursing a fat goose egg on the back of my skull. Gradually the room came into focus. My arms looked different. My clothes looked different, too. I gave myself a thorough going over.

It dawned on me that I was wearing the same outfit I wore with the Indian Alley Gang, 25 years ago. That was impossible. I'm six three and over 200 pounds. No way would I fit into that getup now.

Yet, there I was, looking like a dope in my patched pants, suspenders, baggy sweater, and the same floppy newsboy cap I wore in the movies. Even worse, my ankles were shackled and my hands tied in front of me with a piece of rope. I faced a room with three doors. I was on the haunted castle set from *Spooks and Kooks*. This was the one-reeler where we should have been doing our chores at home. Instead, we sneaked into to the local amusement park and left mom in the lurch.

A voice broke the silence. A few words were all it took to recognize their owner — none other than Thorner von Einsburg, or should I say, Arvin Asquith?

"Buster! Let us begin," the voice said. "In this scene, you are very frightened. You are looking for a way out of the room. You go to each of the doors, one by one, left to right and open them. As you open each door, something very frightening jumps out at you. I want you to roll your eyes, open your mouth wide and scream loudly. You are very frightened, *yah*? When you come to the last door on the right, the floor will open beneath you. You fall through the trap door. End of scene. Have you got that, Buster?"

I was still groggy from the sap on my conk; I yelled: "Come out where I can see you, von Einsburg! Or do you prefer Arvin Asquith?"

A figure emerged from behind a bank of lights. He was older now, with a full beard like his deceased twin brother, dressed as I remembered him at Monarch Studios, in jodhpurs, knee high riding boots, a linen shirt with puffy sleeves, red cravat, and his trademark monocle.

"This time I do not want any mistakes! Do you understand me, Buster?"

The noxious Nazi was getting on my last nerve, but I had to take it, like I did when I worked at Monarch.

"Do as I tell you," he continued, "and when we are finished, you and the other children may go to the cafeteria for ice cream. You can have any flavor you wish. Triple scoops this time. That would make you happy, *yah*?"

He may have been a genius in his heyday, but now his brain was as dense as boarding house tapioca. I took a chance and tried reasoning with him.

"Look, Arvin, Iris is in the car. She wants to take you back to San Francisco. Untie me and let's go."

A creepy smile spread across his map.

"Is that what you think, my little smart aleck? I have a surprise for you. Would you like to see it? Please say *guten tag* to my lovely assistant."

Right on cue, she walked onto the set — Iris Asquith! She was the sap who sapped me when I came through the door. I walked into their trap and brought the cheese with me!

"Okay, I'm a first-class dope," I said to Iris. "You were up to your plucked eyebrows in this all along. You two iced Swifty, Sparky, Tubby, and Sniffles."

Von Einsburg interrupted my recriminations.

"Stop! Those are not your lines! Follow my instructions! Because of you stupid brats, they put me in that place, that prison!"

Even an armchair headshrinker could diagnose this chump. He was a nut in search of a squirrel, and I was the squirrel. In von Einsburg's warped world, the Indian Alley Gang was to blame for loosening his screws. Never mind the pressure from Uncle Bud to grind out picture after picture, week after week. Never mind the feud with his brother Onslow to win the charms of the delicate flower, Iris, who, by the way, must have switched sides long ago.

I stalled for time.

"I take it you plan to rub out the entire gang, is that it?"

"*Yah*, that describes the screenplay I wrote in the sanitarium. It is the only thing that kept me going. I have written re-takes of my best scenes. Since you children were never good at following my orders, all you have to do now is die. Simple, *yah*? Even an actor as bad as you can do that."

"At the risk of sounding trite," I said thickly, "you'll never get away with it. By now the cops are on their way. They've figured out you're the brains behind the killings." Von Einsburg seemed unmoved by my theoretical scenario.

"Hah! I take it you have not read the newspapers. The police believe the deaths were accidental, as I planned. I'm afraid they have nothing that points to me or to my lovely assistant."

"You mean, not yet," I said. "This scene won't look that way. Not by a long shot."

"Do not worry yourself, Wonder Boy. You will simply disappear, like Mandark disappeared each night on stage."

I pointed my chin at his deranged damsel. "I suppose black widow over there croaked the real Onslow Asquith?"

With a touch of malevolence Iris replied: "We couldn't have Onslow talking to the police. After you discovered him in the asylum it was only a matter of time. We had to take care of him. Onslow was such a stupid man. I never should have married him."

She was a black widow all right, and as cuckoo as Onslow's evil twin.

I said: "So, you swam to the other side of the gene pool with Arvin. How'd you know he was staying in the asylum as von Einsburg?"

"Oh, we never lost touch, but Onslow didn't know that. I would take the bus to visit Arvin in the asylum. After he finished his new screenplay, we planned his escape, and it worked perfectly. We knew no one would believe Onslow's story, that is, until you showed up."

"Since we're having such fun at our little reunion," I said, "tell me why you iced Bob MacGyver."

"Oh yes, MacGyver," the crazy bird warbled. "He was a wonderful cameraman but a terrible nuisance. You see, we found out he was writing a memoir about his career at Monarch Studios. He even came to Napa to interview Thorner. But this was after we replaced Arvin with Onslow. MacGyver wasn't sure about Onslow's story at first, but after Tubby Manheim's death, MacGyver got suspicious. He was on his way to your office to let the cat out of the bag. And of course you'd believe him, because you were beginning to piece things together."

"He reached me just the same," I rasped. "So, you hired me with a cock and bull story about Onslow's disappearance to lure me into your boyfriend's screenplay. You were the cameraman at Sniffles' soap bubble scene in Santa Cruz, and for all the other murder scenes."

"You've finally caught on," the vulture chuckled. "Lucky for us, you didn't catch on fast enough. You were so distracted by your dead friends that we were afraid we'd never get around to filming your scene."

I said: "And you slipped each one of the gang a Mickey before filming their scenes, just like Arvin drugged Onslow. You're a real pair of sickos."

Von Einsburg cut off my denouement.

"Enough! We are wasting valuable time."

He cleaned his monocle with a handkerchief, and popped it back into his eye. The megaphone went up to his lips.

"Are we ready?" he shouted. "Remember, Buster, go to each door one by one, open them, and look frightened at what you see."

"These shackles are cramping my style," I griped. "And how am I supposed to open doors with my hands tied?"

"Don't worry, young man," the fruitcake replied. "The doors will pop open as you approach them. You will have no problem walking in your shackles."

"Swell," I said. "Let's get this show on the road."

He glanced at his assistant.

"Lights!"

I heard the zap of an electric arc. Two banks of lights came on. These guys must have tapped into an outside power pole. Iris stationed herself behind a Bell and Howell 2709B silent movie camera, clutching the crank in readiness.

Von Einsburg shouted, "Speed!"

Iris began cranking the camera up to speed.

"Action!"

That was my cue. I shuffled my shackles to the first door. It opened as von Einsburg said it would. Behind the door, a skeleton with a five and dime devil mask danced crazily under a single spot light.

Von Einsburg was not pleased. "You do not look frightened enough, Buster! Emote, emote!"

"Are you kidding? This is Oscar material," I grumbled.

I hobbled to the next door. It opened.

A creature with bat wings and a dragon's head reached its hairy mitts out to grab me. Smoke poured from its nostrils; its eyes glowed like red, hot coals. It was the same script von Einsburg used in *Spooks and Kooks*. If I remembered correctly, the third door meant trouble.

As the Asquith cuckoo cranked her camera, von Einsburg raised the megaphone to his frothy lips.

"Now, move to the final door," he ordered. "When you reach the door, the floor will drop and you will fall through a trap door. *Yah?* Action!"

In the original version of *Spooks and Kooks*, a slide under the trap door took me to a gag guillotine. It was our usual morality play ending. I should have been at home helping mother with the dishes instead of carousing with the gang at the fun house.

The door opened. A giant skull, suspended by a wire, came screaming toward me. At the same time, the trap door opened and I dropped two feet below floor level. Von Einsburg was pleased.

"Cut!" he shouted. "It seems your acting has improved, Buster."

"I'll have my agent renegotiate my contract," I grouched.

The two nut jobs pulled me out of the hole.

"Now," von Einsburg explained, "we move on to the final scene where your head is locked in the guillotine. If you recall, in the original film you are expelled through the fun house doors onto the street before the blade cuts your head. We have changed the timing just a little. You are getting the director's cut, so to speak."

It looked like my head had a date with a wicker basket. Von Einsburg and his manic assistant shoved my noggin into the guillotine, locking it in place.

As von Einsburg held a loop to his eye to check his framing, Iris repositioned her 2709B, which, as I recalled, was Chaplin's favorite camera.

"*Yah, sehr gut,*" the phony Kraut muttered. "Speed! Action!"

Von Einsburg reached for the rope that would give me a shave and haircut in one slice. He took it in his right hand, waiting for his cue to give it a yank. I was pondering how Harry Houdini would have done this scene, when I heard a roscoe sneeze from somewhere in the wings.

"KA-CHOW! KA-CHOW!"

Von Einsburg flinched, dropped the rope, and grabbed his left shoulder.

"Cut! Cut!" He hit the floor like a harpooned whale.

Iris Asquith looked on in horror. She stopped cranking the camera and bolted for the door as fast as her gamey gams could haul. Two harness bulls at the door slapped cuffs on her. That's when St. James and his two sidekicks came out of the shadows.

"We heard everything the Heinie and his henchwoman said, Blade. These vampires never cease to amaze me with the nonsense they come up with. What the hell was this cretin thinking?"

St. James reached down, yanked von Einsburg to his feet.

"Okay boys, book this two-bit Stroheim. If he doesn't suck gas in the big Q, I guarantee he'll be milking cows at the nut farm till doomsday; only this time his twin won't be there to swap places with him."

St. James unhitched me from the guillotine.

"As for you, Hawkshaw, if you'd listened to your slant-eyed siren over there, you wouldn't be lying here looking like a newsboy with a hormone condition."

Paloma moved into the light next to St. James. Her jade green peepers were a sea of hot and sour soup, and I was the bozo on the life raft.

"Maybe you'll listen to the yarrow sticks next time, Alex," Paloma said. "I found your filmography, and looked up the movie that came after *Laundry Day*. It was *Spooks and Kooks*, and you were the lead. That's when I called St. James and told him you'd gone to Niles to find Asquith."

"I'm surprised he came," I said. "Niles is out of his territory."

The homicide honcho grinned: "I know the sheriff here. His boys will take good care of Adolf and Eva. I've had a tail on you all week, Philo. But when Paloma told me what you were up to, I thought she might like to come along.

"You know, Buster, the more I think about it," St. James said, "this could have been your big comeback. Grauman's Chinese might have put your feet in cement after all."

I kept my kisser shut.

42
At Last OAHSPE!

Streetlights across San Francisco flickered out as we crossed the Bay Bridge. The sun rose behind us, but sleep was a long way off. I let Paloma pilot the Terraplane, what with my head still pounding from the sap Iris gave me.

Our first stop was police headquarters, where St. James took my statement. After that, we slogged our dogs up the Mayfair's four flights of stairs.

Stan Raycraft heard about the pinch over the police band. He was in the waiting room when we arrived.

"Hi ho, Alex! It's Pulitzer time! I heard St. James was on his way to lay cuffs on your screwy director, or should I say, Arvin Asquith. That's solid, man, you finally tracked him down!"

"He found me, not the other way around," I said. "That fiasco in Niles last night explained everything. Like, why Onslow Asquith snubbed Francie Ferris at the bank that day. It was his evil twin Arvin withdrawing those thousand bucks.

"Nobody knew that Thorner von Einsburg was Arvin Asquith's Hollywood alter ego. After the nervous breakdown, he nursed a grudge on the gang as the root of his problems. Twenty-five years later, he began stalking us while Iris had me running in circles looking for Onslow.

"Arvin wrote a screenplay in the asylum that would be his directorial comeback. St. James recovered film cans in the trunk of Arvin's car with the scenes he'd shot of Swifty, Tubby, Sniffles, and Sparky. My name was on an empty can."

Stan was writing furiously in his reporter's notebook as I rambled.

"Von Einsburg had a real bad case of Hollywood and Vain if you ask me," Stan observed.

I lit a Chesterfield and took a long drag.

"That's right. Everything pointed to someone with an intimate knowledge of our Indian Alley Gang flicks, but no one suspected Arvin. He was Thorner von Einsburg, locked up in the insane asylum."

Paloma was laying out the yarrow sticks again. She'd been listening to our conversation and finally chimed in.

"Alex, did you ever wonder how Luther Brown knew von Einsburg was the key to this case? You know, his story about Cain and Abel did come true."

"Dunno, Angel. Maybe the space brothers were on to something after all."

"The yarrow sticks and even Mr. Ching were onto something, too," she said.

"Yeah, yeah, I've seen the light. I'm a born-again yarrow stick convert now, which reminds me. Where's my copy of OAHSPE? I've turned this place upside down and still can't find it."

"You didn't look hard enough," Paloma said. "It's on top of our television set, next to the black panther TV light."

"The television? No wonder I couldn't find it! That's the last place I would have looked!"

ABOUT THE AUTHOR

Richard Toronto worked as a printer before he taught photography at Napa State Hospital for the Criminally Insane. He graduated with a BA in Journalism and a Photography minor from CSU Sacramento. He studied film at CSU San Francisco but dropped out. His short film, *Creature in My Blood*, screened one night on the Creature Features TV show in Oakland, California.

Nevertheless, television was not in Toronto's future. Instead, he began writing books. There's a list of them on the first page of this one. Read it, and we won't have to reprint them here. His most recent books are his Frisco Detective Mysteries, which take place in post-WWII California.

https://www.facebook.com/Shavertron1/
https://www.facebook.com/the.frisco.detective/
www.shavertron.com
www.friscodetective.com

Before You Go:

It is always appreciated when readers leave reviews for our books on Amazon.com. It's the only way a book gets noticed, for ranking on Amazon. Thanks in advance for the review, be it good, bad, or somewhere in the middle.

Marvin D. Fox
Chief, Cook, Bottle Washer,
You Dirty Rat Books

www.ingramcontent.com/pod-product-compliance
Lightning Source LLC
Chambersburg PA
CBHW052146170626
46812CB00004B/1615